This is a work of fiction. Similarities to real people, places, or events are entirely coincidental.

A MAIL ORDER BRIDE IN WINTER

First edition. July 13, 2021.

Copyright © 2021 Cindy Upton.

ISBN: 979-8215698969

Written by Cindy Upton.

A MAIL ORDER BRIDE IN WINTER

CINDY UPTON

Adeline swiped the tears away. There was nothing she could do about the hand she'd been dealt. If she had been a gambler like her pa, she would have folded by now and called it a day. Not that she'd known much of her pa's gambling ways, he and her ma had been killed when the wagon train had been attacked when she was only five years old, but the tales the wagon master had told her had left an impression. Seeing the mound of fresh dirt on James's grave brought to mind another wave of grief that she thought had long been buried.

She chewed on her lower lip as the memory swept her back in time to her childhood. Her mother had seen the Indian raiders on the hillside and had tucked her in the cedar chest beneath the quilts and set the barrel of flour on top of it. The last thing she heard from her parents was instruction to be quiet and that they loved her. Then, from her muffled hiding place, she heard the war cry. Mercifully, time had dulled that memory and the memories of her first days as an orphan. If it hadn't been for the few surviving adults who had known to look for her, she might have been left for dead herself. She guessed that it was her lot in life to be left behind by her loved ones. When she'd married James, she'd finally found her true home again. Their marriage had been all too brief. Five years was just not enough years in which to pack a lifetime of love. Tears streamed down her face because she was alone and lonely again. The weight of raising her son on her own was a daunting task at best. Preston had been his father's shadow, until the sickness had set in. Adeline pondered her son's lot in life. It was as if her own childhood was being passed on to him. It was not the sort of inheritance a mother desired to pass down to her child. Adeline gripped Preston's hand tighter. The boy didn't squirm under the extra pressure; in fact, he squeezed her hand tighter as tears splashed off his lashes.

Adeline's reflections were interrupted as Andrew took her elbow in his palm. "Adeline, are you ready to go?" His voice held an extra note of tenderness as he spoke. He too was grieving the loss of his beloved friend James.

Adeline nodded, and the trio turned toward the buggy. The circuit riding minister reached out to lift Preston into the buggy. Preston shook his hand free of his mother's as he raised his arms to accept the big man's help. Andrew offered his hand to assist Adeline into the buggy as well. When mother and son were settled into their seats, the two men climbed aboard. The clergyman's buggy led the small procession back to Adeline's humble home. The small house was a far cry from the plantation standards of yesteryear. To the preacher, it appeared to be a lean-to cabin with a couple of rooms added on as an afterthought. To Andrew, it was still a work in progress, but James had hammered his last nail. Andrew knew that he would be the one to help Adeline with the things that James had left undone. He had promised his friend just that on his deathbed just a few days ago, but Adeline was not aware of it. Andrew had spared Adeline at the sickbed by sitting with his friend so that she could nap. Adeline was never gone from James for long, but Andrew had assured James that Adeline could not hear their private conversations about who would care for her after he was gone. Adeline would have protested the need for it; both men had been sure of that.

There were few women living in the Territory. Adeline only had a couple of close neighbor-women as friends. They were in attendance with their husbands. They brought baskets of food for the after-service meal. They had baked and fixed their finest dishes to help the new widow during her time of grief. They took turns hugging and consoling Adeline and Preston.

After the neighbors had all gone back to their own homesteads and dark was creeping into the corners of the cabin, Adeline sent Preston to his bed. She curled up in her own and wept. The tears rolled down her face in a torrent. When finally the last sob caught in her throat, exhaustion overtook her. She slept.

The next morning, she woke to the sound of the rooster's crow. She pulled the covers over her head and groaned. "I can't do this alone, Lord," she said.

She pulled herself out of bed because life had to go on whether she liked it or not. She scrubbed her face with the cold water and dried with the rough towel. She pinned her hair up in a messy bun in the way that James had always liked for her to wear it. Soft ringlets of brown hair framed her face. She tied on her apron and set to fixing breakfast for her strapping young son. The growing boy had to eat, and he was the reason that she must go on.

The pair settled into a new routine. Preston tried to do things that his Pa had always done. He sat at the head of the table and turned thanks for the meals. He fetched the firewood for the cook stove from the shed. The logs were almost too heavy for him, but he hefted them with all his might. It was one less thing his mother would have to do. She had taken up the slack in plowing and working in the fields. Although Andrew had dropped by on occasion, Adeline had repeatedly assured him that she didn't need his help, and from what he could see, she was right. She was handling it all, but it hadn't completely deterred Andrew from stopping over. He dropped by with candy for the boy and to do a few odd jobs that he noticed needed doing.

It was on a clear fall day that Andrew dropped by to honor his promise to his friend. Keeping an eye on Adeline and Preston was all James had asked, and Andrew hadn't forgotten his pledge to honor that promise until Adeline found another husband. She had been so devoted to James that Andrew doubted another man could ever turn her head. Andrew had often entertained the idea of placing an ad for a mail order bride, but with Adeline and Preston , Andrew had decided to hold off on that. They were his priority for now.

As Andrew climbed off his horse, Preston came out of the barn. "Hi, Mr. Andrew," he said.

There was something about the boy that tugged at Andrew's heart strings. "Hello, Preston. You're looking mighty fine this morning."

"Thank you, sir," he said.

Andrew expected Adeline to walk out of the cabin, but she didn't. "Where's your ma?"

"She's out plowing. I was supposed to be inside the cabin, but I wanted to help. I was mucking out the stalls and putting corn in the crib."

"Those are big chores for a fellow your size," Andrew observed.

"Not too big for me," Preston said with his shoulders squared proudly. "I'm the man of the house now."

"Yes, you certainly are." Andrew agreed. "I'm going to take over the plowing for your ma. That's not work fit for a lady."

"Ma says she is both Ma and Pa now so she is doing things she never has done before," Preston told him.

Andrew nodded. "She's doing it all well, but she doesn't have to do it today."

Preston nodded and fell into step beside Andrew, taking four steps to Andrew's one, as they walked to the field. Andrew whistled loudly for Adeline. The mules paused in their tracks as she turned to look over her shoulder at the unfamiliar whistle. "Wait here for your Ma," Andrew told Preston. Preston nodded and stopped.

Andrew covered the ground in no time to take the reins of the plow out of Adeline's scraped and worn hands. "I'm plowing today," he said.

Adeline was flustered by Andrew's take charge attitude, but if her neighbor wanted to do her plowing for her, she wasn't going to put much effort into arguing. Laboring on the farm as a widow was not how she'd envisioned her life. "You don't have to do that," she said.

"I know, but I'm here and able," he said.

Adeline smiled her thanks. "I'll go inside and fix you a decent meal for your trouble."

"That's mighty kind of you, but you don't have to do it," he replied.

"Least I can do," she said.

Adeline scurried to the cabin to whip up a quick meal. She had plenty of meat and stores packed away. James had been a good provider and a good shot. He provided plenty of venison. He also raised beef cattle and hogs. The smokehouse was full, and they had been eating from it in the months since his passing. It would likely last them until the end of the year, but soon they would have to start replenishing their supply. Adeline pulled the biscuits out of the oven and placed the food on the table. She sent Preston to fetch Andrew from the field.

Preston ran full steam ahead to the field. Having a visitor for the noon meal had always been a rare occurrence, and he could not wait to sit and listen to the man talk. He had missed the conversations at the table. His ma and pa had always chattered over the meals, but since his pa's funeral, his ma had been entirely too quiet for Preston's liking. She talked to him when she had to, but there was no joy in her eyes. Preston hoped that Mr. Andrew could bring that joy light back into his ma's eyes.

Preston slowed to a stop at the end of the row. Mr. Andrew was half way down the last row and headed to him. Preston waved a hand. Mr. Andrew nodded. When Andrew reached the end of the row, he threw the reins on the plow and unhitched the mule team from its burden. "Ma has food on the table. She sent me to fetch you," he said.

"Good thing! I'm starved for a good meal. I get tired of my own cooking," Andrew replied.

"Ma is a good cook. I bet she'd cook for you anytime you wanted," Preston told him.

"I wouldn't want to put her to any extra trouble," Andrew said as the pair hurried toward the cabin's wash basin. Andrew took out his red handkerchief and mopped the sweat beaded on his brow.

"No extra trouble, sir, she still cooks enough to feed three," he said.

The pair washed off in the basin with Preston standing on a step stool to reach it. Andrew sniffed the air appreciatively. The aroma of freshly fried ham was in the air, and he sniffed again. The smell of smoke was in the air also. He turned to look for the cause. On the horizon, he spotted a plume of smoke. He couldn't gauge how far away it was, but it hadn't been there two hours ago when he'd ridden to the farm. He wrote it off as nothing and went inside to eat.

Andrew was fairly new to the prairie. Where he grew up in the foothills of the Ozarks, wildfires would have to jump creeks and dirt trails to destroy to homes, but on the prairie fires were destructive and dangerous because there was nothing to stop them. While they were inside eating, the demon fire was eating the dry grass on its way toward them. Before they had eaten the last bite on their plates, the smell of smoke became heavier in the air.

Adeline sneezed. "I smell smoke," she said.

Andrew wrinkled his nose. "I guess the fire is getting closer than I thought," he said.

"Fire?" Adeline asked, alarm in her voice.

Preston nodded. "We saw the smoke when we washed up."

With haste, Adeline pushed back her chair. The screech of the chair's legs on the wood floor was like nails on a chalkboard. It sent chills down their spines before it overturned and landed with a thud. She dashed out the doorway and screamed, "NO!"

What had been a plume of smoke in the distance had become a billowing cloud of smoke. "Draw water in the pails and dash it on the roof!"

Andrew and Preston gathered the pails that were hanging on nails outside the barn for milking. Preston ran for the well. He pushed the well bucket down into the well. Andrew was right behind him. "Let me do this, son."

Preston moved out of the way. Andrew drew up the well bucket and poured the water into the first pail. He knew it was too heavy for the boy if it was filled to the brim, so he didn't quite fill it up. Preston carried the first pail of water to his mother. She pitched the water onto the roof, as high as it would go, and then, she handed the empty pail back to her son. Preston took the empty pail back to Andrew who had two pails ready for him. Preston walked as fast as he could with the pails of water. His mother dashed the water onto the walls and onto the roof. Then, she poured water around the perimeter of the homestead, attempting to form a fire-line around the cabin and barn.

The minutes turned to an hour as they continued to work to preserve the homestead. Adeline kept watch toward the fire. The billowing smoke and ash was looming closer. Stray bits of ash drifted down on top of them. It was Adeline's fear that one lone ember would cause a blaze. She'd heard tales of it happening before, and it was fear that kept her moving when her arms felt as if they were made of lead. She had faith that God would spare their lives, but she didn't want to lose her home that she'd made with James.

As the firestorm neared, she told Andrew to turn all of the animals loose. The horses would surely be able to outrun the blaze. The neighbors would help round them up later if it was necessary, but for now their safety was her first concern. The nearing fire had already alarmed the birds and wildlife. Flocks of birds circled overhead. Their cries of distress were heard above the roaring of the flames. When it became apparent that they had done all that they could do, Andrew called to Adeline, "We have to get in the creek to save ourselves."

Adeline hoped that the water they had poured would slow the fire, but she gathered clothes and quilts into a bundle. The things that she didn't want destroyed in the fire that water wouldn't hurt, she took with her to the creek. Preston gathered his clothing and a few articles belonging to his pa and followed his mother out the door to the creek.

They sat in the creek bed and waited for the monster to chew its way over their heads. As the flames neared them, the trio began to pray. "Duck under," Adeline said.

They sucked in air and dove under the water just in time for the flames to cross the creek. The burned out swath smoldered in its wake. They climbed out of the water unscathed but soggy. They picked a path through the smoldering ashes to check on the cabin. The cabin that James had labored over was no longer recognizable. When Adeline took in the sight of her beloved home, sobs wracked her body. She couldn't contain the howl of horror that emanated from her being. The loss was just too great to bear. She fell to her knees and wept. The ashes and soot left behind from the wildfire coated her and rendered her an ashen hue.

Andrew couldn't look away. He stood as if transfixed on the sight before him. Preston stood still as a statue. His body betrayed him as tears trekked down his cheeks. He was trying to be the man of the house, but now his boyhood home was gone. He was aware that the cabin was not a safe haven for them anymore, and instant panic ripped at his insides. "Ma, where will we live?" The panic in his voice brought Adeline to her feet.

"I don't know, honey. I guess we'll camp outside tonight."

Andrew's jaw dropped in disbelief. "No. If my house is still standing, you'll be staying with me."

Adeline hadn't even considered that Andrew's home might have been in the path of the wildfire too. He'd unselfishly helped them instead of worrying about his own homestead and livestock. She only hoped that the wildfire hadn't split at the creek and had bypassed his homestead. She wasn't hoping that for them, but for him. "Oh, Andrew! I never even thought about your homestead."

He shrugged it off. "Don't worry yourself over it, Adeline. I believe the wildfire missed my place. I just wish it had missed yours too."

She nodded.

"Are you ready to go to my cabin and clean up?"

She wasn't really ready to leave her home behind, but she couldn't justify staying until sundown. "I'm ready."

The horses were running wild, but at Andrew's shrill whistle, they came running. He said, "I guess we'll all be riding since the wagon didn't survive."

Adeline hadn't ridden anything but sidesaddle since she'd married James, but in her younger days, she'd ridden bareback like the boys. "Give me just a minute," she said as she disappeared behind the burned out cabin. She pulled the least soggy pair of James's pants out of the bundle. She pulled them on beneath her skirt. She'd be covered and could ride astride the horse.

When she came back to the horse, she jumped up and caught the horse in the flank and hoisted herself up. Andrew couldn't help but laugh. He'd never seen a grown woman mount a horse in such a way.

She shook her head at his laughter. "What you never saw a woman do that?"

"No indeed!" he replied as he hefted Preston onto the horse he was to ride, and with a swift movement, he swung up on his own stallion.

The ride to Andrew's homestead took longer because they didn't get above a walk. The horses had already had a workout outrunning the fire, and there was no great hurry to get to his homestead. They were all quiet on the way. Not even the breathtaking sunset on the horizon could lift the heaviness surrounding the trio.

As they crossed onto Andrew's property, the stench of the fire lessened. Andrew's cabin was small by many standards, but the loft would be a quiet place for Adeline to rest. He would make a pallet on the floor for young Preston. Although it was improper for a lady to spend the night in a cabin with a man she wasn't married to, Andrew figured that under the circumstances, Adeline's reputation would be protected.

Adeline dismounted and rinsed off at the wash basin. After the males had followed suit, Andrew led her to the loft. "You'll find a bed up there."

"Thank you for letting us stay tonight. We'll figure something out and get out of your hair tomorrow," she said.

"There's no need to rush away," he said.

Adeline shook her head. "I don't know what we'll do for sure when we get there, but we'll go home to our homestead tomorrow."

Andrew realized that arguing with Adeline was fruitless for the evening. He would pray about it tonight.

Once Adeline was in her spot upstairs and Preston was down for the night, Andrew picked up his Bible and began to read. He prayed over the situation. He began to see the situation from a different perspective. He'd been praying for a wife. Adeline needed the protection and shelter of a husband. The story of Boaz and Ruth seemed to be playing out before him. He could help Adeline as the kinsman redeemer. He could give her a home, food, and brotherly love. He decided to talk it over with her in the morning.

When he woke in the morning, Adeline was standing over the stove boiling water for coffee and heating a pan for frying eggs. "Did I wake you?" she asked timidly.

"No, ma'am. It was time for me to rise and shine. You don't have to be cooking, but I'm glad you are!" he chuckled.

Adeline laughed. "I like an honest man," she said.

The sound tickled Andrew's ears.

"You won't find one more honest than me," he replied as he pulled up a chair. He turned it around and placed his arms on the back as he sat. "I been thinking about the Book of Ruth."

Adeline turned to look at him with a frown. "Huh?"

"You being like Ruth. And me being like Boaz."

"Huh." Adeline muttered as she flipped an egg.

Andrew wasn't sure how to continue, so he didn't. Adeline continued cooking. After it became clear to Adeline that Andrew was not going to say more, she said, "Ruth and Boaz?"

"You know in the Bible. The Book of Ruth."

Adeline had little formal schooling and church had not been high on the list of priorities with the Reardens who raised her. They had been of good moral character, but she had never heard them quote scripture. James had been the one to really introduce her to the Bible by reading aloud at bedtime, but she didn't recall the book Andrew mentioned. "No."

Andrew frowned. He'd been fairly sure that Adeline was a follower of Christ since she'd insisted that the circuit-riding preacher be summoned for James's Christian burial. He raked a hand through his hair. Surely James had not been unequally yoked with an unbeliever. "Well, there's a book in the Old Testament about Ruth."

"Oh."

Andrew decided to change the course of the conversation. "After the chores are through, we'll read it together, if you'd like."

"That would be pleasant," she said.

He chose his words carefully. "You see, I was thinking that you and Preston could stay on here. I have been wanting a wife. Preston needs a pa. . ., and if we were married, nobody could talk badly about you living here."

Adeline was shocked by his suggestion. "You mean a marriage without love?"

Andrew said, "It would be a love born of respect between us."

Adeline was sure that the neighbors would suggest she live with another couple rather than with Andrew, but living with the others didn't appeal to her at all. They all had all they could handle under their own roofs. She felt sure that living with Andrew was the only possible solution, and living with a man she wasn't married to was not really an option at all. As she mulled it over, his suggestion that they marry for convenience was the only possible solution. "It seems to be a good solution, but only until spring. After winter is over and the cabin is repaired, we will go back to being neighbors."

Andrew nodded. "We'll marry when the preacher makes his rounds."

Adeline nodded. "And, we'll divorce when the calves are born in spring. But, be sure to read that story to me later."

Andrew was sure that God had placed Adeline in his life for more than just a season, and maybe it was a part of His plan to make sure that Preston continued to learn of God at a young age. Since James had been the spiritual leader of the household, it was now falling on Andrew's broad shoulders to do the same. "We'll read it together as a family," Andrew said.

The word 'family' struck a chord deep inside Adeline. Family was something she'd longed for—a place to belong; a place of love as she remembered it ever so dimly. She'd had the security of family with James, and now, in her darkest moment of need since childhood, Andrew offered that security to her and to Preston, but a loveless marriage was not how she'd envisioned her married life. She remembered the affectionate touches exchanged between her parents and between herself and James. A loveless marriage with a kind man would be better than the home she had as a child. It had been a hard life for them all. She'd been looked at as another pair of hands to work on building the homestead. It was what had made her no stranger to hard work on their own homestead. She'd do no less for Andrew. If she and Preston had been home alone; she shuddered at the thought. Sleeping on the ashen ground would have been their lot. She pondered that for a moment. Andrew patterned his life after the Savior, and it was no wonder that he had been their savior in their time of need.

She mopped and swept the planks on the hardwood floor. The mud in the pail made it appear as if he had never mopped or swept before. Andrew and Preston handled the manly chores that Adeline had been doing on her own since James's illness and subsequent death, and Adeline continued to turn the bachelor cabin into a home. After the mopping and scrubbing, Adeline took down the lone curtain and washed it in a pail of clean water. The water quickly turned the pail a sooty gray and mud brown color. There was nothing worse than a home without a woman's touch, she mused. It wouldn't take long for her to set the place to right with a homey touch. A candle here and there, and a lace doily for the tabletop. She'd learned from Mrs. Rearden how a home should look. Mrs. Rearden had been reared in a high society family in Boston, and the sophisticated touches had transformed the shanties they lived in from a mere dwelling to a home. Those little homey touches had been the difference that her own mother had known about, but hadn't lived long enough to teach Adeline herself. The cedar chest she'd hidden in had held those same treasures. A tear dripped down her cheek. She hoped that the cedar chest was intact in the burned out shell of her former home. It would be a miracle if it was.

With a bit of time between spent between chores, she had time to digest all that had happened over the last few weeks. Time alone had been at a premium since Preston was never far from her sight. With him shadowing Andrew there was nothing to distract her from her sorrow. Tears streamed down her face. Minutes turned to an hour, and the sobs turned to sniffles. She didn't know what the future held, but she knew one thing, she was strong enough to survive it all.

She walked outside to see what was in the smokehouse for supper. She was pleased to see that the smokehouse here was nearly full. Combining the smokehouses from both properties would last them through the winter, and they wouldn't have a need for Andrew to be spending time hunting for food. Meat was plentiful now. She sighed; thankful for good meals to be prepared for her family. She pulled down the venison and cut out a hunk for stew. Next, she found vegetables covered in the corner of the root cellar. She pulled out enough to make a hearty meal. She wrapped them up in her white apron. Then, she trudged back to the cabin where she washed them in the wash basin. She left them to soak while she went to fetch the big stew pot. She pulled them out and plopped them into the big pot. Pouring water into the big pot, she covered the vegetables. Then, she sprinkled herbs and spices on top of it. She hefted the big pot and wagged it inside to place on the stove to boil. She had supper handled with one pot. She smiled and dusted her hands together. A good meal always made things better.

As she settled into the rocking chair, she heard the rattle of a buggy down the lane. She crept to the window to peer outside. She looked down at the black dress and stained white apron. She wasn't dressed fit for company. She saw that it was the circuit-riding preacher. She clapped a hand over her mouth. Argh! Getting married in this awful rag! She ran to the ladder to climb up into the loft to see if she'd brought anything worth wearing. She knew she only had a few moments before he would be knocking at the door. It didn't take long to sort through the small bundle of clothes she'd gathered. All she'd grabbed were widows' weeds, save one lone dress—her wedding dress that she'd worn when she'd married James. She didn't want to seem presumptuous, so she climbed back down the ladder to the main room of the cabin still dressed in the worn black day dress.

When the knock at the door came, she walked over and opened it. "Hello."

The preacher smiled. "I'm so glad to see you here!"

"You must've been by our place," she guessed.

"Yes indeed! I went there to spend a little time with you and the boy. . . . When I didn't find you at home, I was afraid you had been taken unaware."

"If it hadn't been for Andrew, we would have been there alone, but he had stopped by to help with the plowing before the wildfire broke out."

"Praise be! I'm glad you weren't alone! Scary enough with another body, but aww my I can only imagine by one's self how terrifying that would have been," he said as the door whooshed open behind him allowing Preston and Andrew to enter.

Preston lay down on the pallet in the corner to listen to the grown folks. He found that he learned more by listening at a distance than he did if he was in the middle of the conversation. Andrew sat in the chair opposite the preacher. "You'll stay for dinner with us, won't ye, Parson?"

"I'd be much obliged for a plate," he said.

"There's something Adeline and I wanted to discuss with you. Did she tell you?" Andrew asked.

"Why, no. We were just chatting about the fire yesterday."

"Well, it's about that," he said. "With Adeline and Preston staying on here, we think it is best if we marry."

"Marry?" asked the preacher with a glance at Adeline.

Preston's ears perked up at the word. He smiled. His prayers were answered!

"Yes, sir," Adeline confirmed.

It had only been six months since James's death, but it wasn't unusual for folks to marry again so the preacher nodded. "If you'd like to get married, I'll do the ceremony for you."

"Thank you!" Andrew smiled.

"May I go change first?" Adeline asked.

"Yes, indeed! We can do the ceremony and have supper after," he agreed.

Adeline went upstairs to pretty herself up. She'd no longer be needing the widows' weeds. She brushed out her brown hair and let it flow down her back. She was already flushed from the idea of being married so she didn't even need to pinch her cheeks to make them pink. She pulled the wedding dress over her head, and with fumbling fingers fastened the dress's buttons. With only a few moments left as a widow, she took a deep breath and climbed down the ladder again.

Andrew had never seen a woman as lovely as the vision before him. He'd never really looked at Adeline when she had been James's wife, but as she was his bride standing before him, he was awed by her beauty. "Aww, Addie! You are beautiful!"

The compliment stole Addie's heart, raw though it was with pain and sorrow. She feared that she wouldn't want to give him up when spring arrived.

The ceremony was brief, but Andrew was delighted to seal it with a kiss. He'd always prayed for a lovely bride, and at long last, God had answered that prayer. He knew Adeline had said that she only wanted to be married for the next season of life, but he hoped by March to have changed her mind about leaving. She was beautiful and sweet of spirit.

After supper was dished up into bowls, the foursome gathered at the table. The preacher turned thanks and blessed the new union. Though he knew they said it was a marriage of convenience, he had seen the looks on their faces during the ceremony. He was expecting them to grow old together.

Adeline intended to keep to her bed in the loft, but decided against it because she didn't want Preston to get the wrong idea. She wanted Preston to see them as a happily married couple, even if it was a marriage of convenience.

During the first week as husband and wife, Adeline settled into the familiar routine of housekeeping and cooking. Andrew was free with his compliments and set in his ways of doing chores. He and Preston were fast friends, and Preston was happy to follow along behind Andrew's footsteps. Andrew was surprised at how much help the boy was at such a young age. The day's work was done in three-quarters the time. The amount of responsibility weighted on his shoulders at a young age had formed the boy into a hardworking young man. He was proud to call him son, even if he wasn't his by blood.

A month rolled by, and the circuit riding preacher came round. Adeline invited him for the Thanksgiving meal. He agreed. While Andrew and Preston entertained the preacher, Adeline climbed up the ladder to prepare the bed with clean bedding. When she heard the group singing hymns below, she smiled and closed her eyes. Life had never been sweeter to her this year, than in this moment. She had much to be thankful for.

Every month, he dropped by to see how things were going with the couple. He could see that they were growing close. When Andrew walked out with him, he asked, "Are you still planning to split up in spring?"

"I hope not," he said.

The preacher went on his way and kept the pair in his prayers.

Andrew, Preston, and Adeline rode into town to pick up supplies. While Adeline was in the mercantile picking out material for new clothing for them all, Andrew and Preston carried out the feed and seed. They were stacking the wagon and did not see the man with the bandanna over his face walk down the boardwalk and into the mercantile. Adeline had her back to the doorway, unfolding a bolt of cloth.

William, the owner of the mercantile, did not look away from Adeline when the bell above the door jangled. He said, "Come on in. Be with you in a minute."

"You'll be with me, now!" the masked man replied. He had a gun in hand and waved it at the older man.

Adeline turned to look over her shoulder. She screamed when she saw the gun pointed at William. The masked man waved the pistol in her direction, and she screamed again. Andrew heard Addie's shrill screams, and he ran to the mercantile. He looked through the window and saw the man with the gun. It was clear that his Addie was in danger, and he was not going to leave the matter to the local lawman. He opened the door quickly and covered the distance between himself and the gunman in two strides. He grabbed the man's gun arm and wrenched the gun from his hand. It dropped to the floor with a thud. Adeline reached down to grab it, but Andrew had already kicked it out of reach of the masked man. The masked man tried to squirm free of Andrew's grasp, but Andrew was stronger. He had been wrestling with calves much more slippery than the man, and he had him firmly in hand. He said, "William, go get the lawman. I've got this coyote."

William went out the back way to fetch the sheriff. He wasn't gone long, and they returned to retrieve the outlaw. When the sheriff took the bandanna off the man's face, he whistled. "You just got yourself a reward! You have just apprehended one of the most wanted men on this side of the Mississippi."

Preston walked in just in time to hear about the reward. "Pa, you're Ma's hero!"

Once the sheriff had the man in custody and on his way to the jailhouse, Addie grabbed Andrew in a hug. He leaned down and kissed her. It was their very first kiss on the lips. "You're my hero, Drew!"

With that first flawless kiss, it was clear to them both that they had grown a love during the winter season that would last a lifetime.

LET THERE BE LOVE

BONNIE WILLIAMS

The man in front of her looked worse every day. Henry Whitwood was a man in his fifties, but he had always seemed like a strapping youngster to Vera with his endless supply of vigor. That was before he caught something nasty. It had only been a few days ago that he started looking weak, and by now he already looked ready to fall over.

Vera tried to help by making him some soothing herbal tea. However, with Henry's illness also came a serious loss of appetite. The man hadn't touched food since he picked Vera up from the Romanov-on-Murman port. Right now he was even unable to stand. He sat down on a closed barrel of wine, looking out at sea with a pained expression on his face. Vera sat on the floor, her long black skirt fluttering in the wind despite her attempts to keep it still. Her hair received similar abuse thanks to the rough sea. She would have bristled yarn for hair by the time they reached America.

She was afraid that making any noise would make his headache worse. So she just silently looked out at sea, smelling the salty air all around her. Minutes ticked by with each breath, and Vera counted each one. She could be sewing a new dress right about now, but her concern for her friend took away all her attention.

"How's your head fairing?" she asked in her thick accent.

For a long while she received no response. He must've fallen asleep. She pulled out a piece of parchment from the folds of her dress and began to read. The sender told her of great tales about cowboys fighting the natives, the hot sun that shone all year long, and the bright yellow corn that bore fruit in the summer. In return she told him what her country was like. He responded that he would like to see it one day. This was just one of many, many letters he written to her.

Both Vera Zykov and Liam Whitwood both suffered from lack of family. Both had a love of learning about the world. Both had a desire to find their soul mate. They were like two missing puzzle pieces that found each other over seas. That was why Vera was on this boat right now, following Liam's uncle to America.

The old man stirred, "Did you say something, dear?"

"I asked how you were feeling."

"Better, I think," the man winced, "Then again, maybe not."

"You shouldn't push yourself, sir. Your illness will only get worse if you do."

"I'm fine, Bepa," he laughed at their little inside joke. When signing onboard, Vera had accidentally spelled half her name in Cyrillic. The man who read it out loud pronounced it like an American, with R as P and V as B. Vera had been embarrassed at first. However, her friend's laughter soon became contagious, until even she cracked a smile at the nickname.

Vera decided to change the topic.

"Mr. Whitwood. Why didn't you let Liam on board? He told me in his letter that he wanted to be the one to see me."

Henry slowly tilted his head toward her, the shadows etching along his laugh lines made him look like a portrait than a real human being. His skin had become so sickly that it almost looked to her like paint.

"Because I have all the experience as a sailor. And he has all the youth. I told him...I said he needed to stay at the farm so that we had food when we got back. He wasn't happy. No siree. But he knew that I had a point."

Vera fell silent, causing Henry to give her a curious look.

"Is something on your mind?"

"Huh? Oh no, sir." In all honesty, she had a lot on her mind. What if there was no Liam Whitwood? Or what if he was already married?

What if he was nothing like his letters described?

Vera knew it was foolish to question herself now. She was already out at sea, well on her way to another country that she had never been to before. She knew going in how much of a gamble she was taking by following Henry.

It was either take a gamble in order to marry for love, or stay where she would be doomed to marry someone she didn't. She knew that she could love no one in her town as well as she loved the man in her letters. Something about how Liam wrote showed sincerity and kindness. Truly that wasn't something a fake man could fabricate.

.....Right?

They watched the sun as his set on the horizon, shading in the sky with golds and purples. Vera sat by Henry's side as they took this journey together.

Days passed with Vera witnessing things she could only have dreamed about before. They got off the port and took a horse to Virginia. She saw what they meant by the wild west. Unlike her city that was filled with people and frost, this place was filled with sand and wide open spaces. They would be on the horse for an entire day without coming across a single other person.

Henry ate, but only from Vera's prodding. He regained a little bit of strength. Finally, they arrived to the Virginian town known as Sungale.

Sungale was barely a few years old as an established location, and Vera could quickly see that. They had only come across a few buildings that seemed miles apart from each other. According to Henry, this spot used to be reserved for hunting, which was why it had remained untouched as a town for so long. In the end, it seemed that the Americans decided they needed more places to live.

Looking at it, Vera was awed by how close to nature this little town was. It was like something out of one of her fairytale books that she had when she was younger: long, yellow wheat, cows and bison wandering the earth, and a dirt road that was barely paved by human hands.

The dust itched at her nose, causing her eyes to water. She managed to avoid sneezing. Henry, on the other hand, didn't fare nearly as well. As soon as they got into town, he began coughing a lung out.

"You must be sick," Vera said.

"Nothing a little time won't cure," he stated between gasps, "Thank you for your concern."

He meant that to be the end of the discussion. Vera reluctantly let it slide, even though her worry grew.

Finally, they happened upon a small wooden house that would just barely house three people. Despite its size, Vera loved it immediately. Its humbleness matched the surrounding area. And it wasn't as though there hadn't been any effort put in to making it look like a house. The roof had been outlined with blue paint that matched the sky. The windows looked brand new. But what most charmed Vera was the small door that had the same color as the roof's exterior. It also had a knob that was painted golden yellow in a way that reminded Vera of the wheat fields.

She found herself enchanted. Despite how tired her bones were from the long distance traveling, she hurried off the horse and led it to the watering hole, where it gave itself a much deserved drink. Henry steadily got off after her, not in his usual energetic way when he would deliver letters to her, but in a slow, pained way.

He motioned for her to follow him. Her heart drummed as they entered the house. A man in his early twenties sat in the living room, polishing a hunting rifle. He took one look at her and stopped what he was doing. Gulping, Vera just inspected him in silence.

At least he looked just as his letters described. Black hair, grey eyes, a little lanky for someone of his occupation, and tiny freckles across his tanned cheeks. A cowboy hat sat right beside him on the table.

The man stood up as soon as they entered. He looked at Vera, who could only stare back. What did you say to a man you're engaged to, and you've only just met?

"Um...hello," she greeted uncertainly.

Liam took a hold of her hand and placed it against her lips. In their letters they spoke of how they enjoyed reading about castles, kings, love and war. Vera immediately knew that this was his way to make her feel welcomed. Her lips spread into a soft smile. He stared up at her.

"It's very nice to finally see you in person."

"Then you really are Liam."

"Yes. And you're no doubt Vera."

"How are you so sure?"

"You're exactly as your letters described. And I knew when writing to you that I was speaking to someone honest."

"Thank you," Vera smiled, feeling partially relieved and partially awkward. This was going to take some time to get adjusted to. Even for things like love, results didn't usually happen overnight.

"How are you feeling, Uncle Henry?" Liam turned to the old man. Henry crouched down on the chair and sighed.

"Just a little tired from the trip."

"You sure? You're looking pale."

"I told him that he needed some rest," Vera pointed out to her finance.

Henry, realizing that he was just about to get tag teamed, immediately changed the topic. He motioned toward his left.

"I see you finished her gift."

He was pointing at a rocking chair that Vera didn't notice before. Now that she got a better look, she noticed the intricate feminine details that stated this seat was for a woman. Flower designs went in curls across the polished wood.

"I was so excited about meeting you that I made you a chair. Though I should've waited until you got here. I didn't realize how small you were," Liam admitted, sounding ashamed.

It was true that Vera was almost a mouse compared to these two men in the room. And although the chair was closer to her size than theirs, it was still a little big. In all honesty, Vera was the smallest woman of her age back in Russia.

"Thank you, Liam. I love it."

The two looked at each other for a long while. However, the silence wasn't that tense. The longer she studied Liam, the more relaxed she became. Now that she knew that he was real and exactly as he said he was, she felt much better about her decision.

Vera and Henry spent the rest of the day recovering from their long trip. By morning, Vera was already making breakfast and Liam was out watering the crops. He didn't return until late morning, and Henry still hadn't gotten out of bed. Vera was setting the table when she noticed this.

"You don't suppose that his illness has gotten worse?"

Liam tried to smile reassuringly, but she could sense a trace of concern drifting through his eyes.

"Let me see if I can wake him up. I'll be right back."

Vera had already got everything on the table by the time she realized that Liam had not returned. A sinking feeling sprouted inside her chest. She made a move to head down the hallway, but stopped when she saw Liam approaching. His smile was more convincing this time around.

"I think his old age has made him more tired. He wouldn't wake up no matter how much I tried. I figured I would just let him sleep 'til he woke."

Vera nodded. She masked her concern with a pleasant smile, just like she was taught to do in Russia. Husbands wanted happy working wives, no matter how bleak the situation might seem.

Despite her efforts, it seemed that Liam caught onto her worry. He proposed that they go into town after breakfast.

"But what about your uncle?" she couldn't help but ask.

"Uncle Henry's always been tough as nails. I doubt a little cold will keep him bedridden for long."

But what if it's not a cold?

Vera kept her thoughts to herself. The last thing she wanted to do was cause him more concern than necessary.

"Alright. If you're sure that he'll be fine by himself. What do you need in town?"

"I wanted to introduce you," Liam said, "It can get lonely here in this little farm. And you told me how much you love company. I wanted to see if you can find some friends."

"That's very kind of you. But I have you now....don't I?" she averted her gaze. Why was she still worried about this? Why did she still have doubts that this path of love would lead to her happiness? Hadn't she felt it in her heart that this was the right choice?

He took her hand into his. It was almost twice the size of hers. Liam wasn't what she would call a big man, however. Vera realized how small she really was.

She looked up at her fiancé's eyes. His pink lips spread into a kind smile, his blue eyes glistening with pleasure. It was as if simply looking at her brought him great joy. Vera couldn't help but smile back.

"You will always have me. Like I said in the letters, I know how much you're sacrificing to come here."

"You're sacrificing a lot too," she pointed out, "You told me that you left your home to be in this farm."

"That's true. But I have Uncle Henry. You only just got here. I don't want you to feel like you're alone. And I know some women in town that like to talk with each other a lot. So I figured...." he trailed off. Vera finished his thought for him.

"I understand. I think it's a splendid idea having some female friends. Do you get along with the men in town?"

"Most of them," Liam smiled, "They're all the same as me. Guys who work with their hands. You won't find too many rich folk here, as this town is mostly people starting all over with their lives. Making new buildings, plowing new fields....it's not as easy as some people dream about."

"Maybe that's why it's so romantic. All the hard work one person can do," Vera said more to herself than to her fiancé.

They rode the farm's horse into town. Vera pressed herself against Liam's back, the summer sun making her sleepy. It would take her a while to get used to this heat.

Sungale looked more like a marketplace than the entire town. The bank, sheriff's office, library, school and shops were all in this one small area. Their horse suddenly found a certain spot of grass that must've been different from the others, for it stopped to have itself a snack.

Liam got off and helped Vera down as well, gently placing her feet on the soft ground. A few people approached them with curious looks on their faces.

"Who we got here, Liam?" a man asked.

"Is she new here?" a woman asked another woman.

Someone turned to Liam with a knowing eye.

"I see you found your soul mate."

Vera paused at those sudden choice of words. True, she did believe Liam was meant to be with her. But how did this man know that?

Liam wrapped his arms around her.

"You're right, Orwell. This is Vera, everybody. We've been writing to each other for a few years."

"Vera?" one of the woman turned up her nose and scoffed, "That doesn't sound very American. Where is she from? Why Liam....there are plenty of good girls within the same country as you. You don't need to go shopping for a bride."

Vera's face warmed with shame. Liam came to her defense.

"She may not be American, Scarlett. But she's one in a million. I doubt that I'd be able to find anybody like her in this country."

Now Vera's cheeks were warm with pleasure. She didn't need any more proof now. This man was everything he was in his letters: courageous, hardworking, and had a way with words. Even Scarlett didn't have a retort for that.

Orwell touched Liam's shoulder.

"Glad you're here. We could use some help getting Earl's cows together. He'll pay us, right Earl?"

They turned to a man with the expression of a lost lamb.

"Um....I'll give you dinner. Is that okay, Orwell?"

The gang laughed, clearly not expecting money in the first place. Vera was awed by their love to help one another. No wonder cowboys could do so much. God smiled on them for their selflessness. For you shall never see a brother's ox fall down and ignore him. How rare it was to see that scripture actually taken to heart.

The girls suddenly got excited. One person grabbed Vera's arm and led her to where they were going to watch. Liam smiled at her. It seemed that she was already making friends.

"What are they doing?" Vera asked the woman whose name she'll later learn as Mary.

"See all the cows around here? The cowboys are going to get them back into that pin over there. They finished grazing, so they need to make sure they don't escape now."

Vera looked to where all the men got on horses. Her Liam had been supplied with a younger, more energetic colt than the one they rode to town on. The horse whinnied in excitement, ready to start sprinting in whatever direction Liam chose.

The men lined up. Orwell issued his order.

"Whoever herds the most wins a drink. Wilder over there's keeping score," he pointed to a teenager with a notepad and a cowboy hat, "Go!"

The girls and Vera watched as the men turned their work into a game. Their horses rushed toward the cows, causing them to sprint away. One cowboy threw a rope that latched onto a horn, throwing the bull right on the ground. The cowboy jumped off his horse in order to tie down the cow's legs.

This was the first time that Vera witnessed real cowboys herding cattle. Her eyes widened in awe at the amazing sight. Something far beyond her imagination could grasp.

She smiled when she saw how Liam already gotten three cows into the pen. He laughed with all the other cowboys, looking like the book definition of merry.

Then something horrifying happened. A rather large bull knocked itself against Orwell's horse. The impact sent the man flying toward the ground. Vera screamed when he landed right on top of his head!

"Goodness, is he okay?" Mary asked. The men had already gathered around Orwell, hiding his body from sight.

No, he wasn't okay, Vera decided. No one could recover from that sort of head trauma. Liam pushed his way through the crowd to check on him. Vera mentally prepared to hear how Orwell was either dead or severely damaged.

To her shock, Liam and Orwell came into view, Orwell looking little more than dazed. There was no hint that anything was broken. The men and women all hurled around them. Vera kept a close eye on the man her fiancé was holding onto.

"Is he alright?" someone from the crowd asked.

"Got the reflexes of a cat," Orwell answered with pride, "I landed feet first on the ground. That helped broke my fall. But now I think I need to sit down for a while."

"You're right. I'll help you. Mary. Vera. Can you two go into Earl's house and fetch some water?" Liam asked.

"I'll help too. We can all make some coffee and cakes," Scarlett announced, ready to please Liam. It got on Vera's nerves.

The gaggle of women went inside the house. It appeared as though Earl would have to buy dinner, since they ended using his ingredients. Vera had little doubt that her fiance would pay the man back.

"You must be really worried," Mary pointed out from behind Vera. She noticed that the Russian woman had been keeping a close eye on Orwell. In truth, Vera had a bad feeling about him. Despite what he said, she knew what she saw. He had landed on his head. He should either be dead or unconscious right now.

Vera took the warnings of the Good Book to heart. She knew there was such a thing as unholy spirits. And she knew they could disguise themselves inside human flesh. But fewer and fewer people believed in such a thing anymore. It would do no good to warn Liam and the others of her suspicions.

She decided to let God help her, remembering what she learned in church. "And he said to them, 'This kind cannot be driven out by anything but prayer.'"

She didn't want to let Mary in on her thoughts.

"You're right. I was shocked to see him stand up after that. Did they catch the bull?"

"Your Liam did. He was always good with animals. Not so much with his crops. When he was a child, he didn't water the wheat enough in the summertime. It nearly caused them to burst in flames. He got into so much trouble. I don't think he ever got the knack for that."

Vera remembered all the produce that their own farm had. Mary's words gave her a sinking feeling. She made a mental note to check on the crops occasionally.

"Dear. Can you bring me some water?" Orwell asked Vera.

The woman froze up on the spot. If Orwell was unnerved by her reaction, he didn't show it. Mary gave her a strange look before grabbing a glass of water herself and bringing it to him.

Vera walked outside. She had just arrived in town and already she was screwing up. Maybe Orwell wasn't a demon. Maybe she had only imagined the injury.

"Bepa?" Liam's voice asked.

Vera stiffened. She faced her fiancé with wide eyes.

"How...?"

"How did I know about that nickname?" Liam chuckled, "Uncle Henry told me in his letters."

Vera averted her gaze. She was still ashamed of herself for the Orwell incident, and now she was embarrassed by the story. Liam took hold of her hand with a soft smile on his face. She smiled back.

"I think it's cute. I'd love to call you that, if that's alright with you."

Vera hugged him, "You may call me whatever you'd like. I'm yours."

"And I'm yours," he whispered inside her ear, "Bepa."

The marriage was beautiful, the reception grand, and the aftermath a happy ending. Months flew by like seconds. Vera was the happiest woman in the world. Her Liam was everything he said he was and more. To her pleasure, it seemed as though he was really trying to learn from his past mistakes with the crops. He would water them at least three times a day, which was especially draining in this intense heat. She made sure to keep him hydrated by bringing him a picture of water whenever he was out in the field. Sweating profusely, the man would always down the entire picture at an impressive speed.

But the good times came to a screeching halt. Henry's illness only gotten worse. They pretty much establish that he had caught yellow fever. He was bedridden since the wedding, and everyday a little more strength left him. Vera held a glass of water to his lips, daintily tilting it down his throat. Liam entered the room, tired from the long hours of work.

"How you doing, ol'timer?"

Henry opened his mouth, but no sound came out.

"I think he lost his voice. He also seems dazed. I don't think he recognizes me."

Liam offers her a comforting smile. It's a lot more forced than usual, "That's probably not true, right uncle? You know Bepa."

His uncle looked at her, or rather, through her. His eyes had some sort of hazy film over them, as if he couldn't process what's going on.

Vera couldn't take that empty stare. She excused herself and made a hasty retreat. She didn't think she could stand to see that look again.

It turned out she didn't have to. Henry died overnight.

At the funeral, Orwell and the others came to pay their respects. Liam held a solemn gaze. The way he looked at the casket unnerved Vera. Something about that expression did not belong to a strong cowboy. It was a lost look. A weak look.

A sturdy hand touched her shoulder. Vera almost screamed when she saw who it was. Orwell leaned closer to her face in order to speak in a soft whisper.

"Liam needs you now more than ever. Make sure you stay by his side."

Vera barely processed what he said. All she could do was stare into the eyes of the monster. She didn't let herself relax until he lifted her hand off her shoulder. His intense gaze stared through her soul, calculating and emotionless.

When he left, Mary came up to her. She was one of the few who approached the mail order bride. Most people had hovered around Liam at the wake. Even Scarlett chatted him up as if this was just a normal party.

"He's really sad," Mary observed.

"Of course. He just lost his uncle."

"I think there's more to it than that."

Vera paused, "What do you mean?"

"Well, you know that his uncle was the only family he had left, right?"

Vera was insulted. She was Liam's wife. Didn't she technically count as 'family?'

Mary continued, oblivious to her friend's displeasure with her remark.

"His uncle was the one who practically raised him. His uncle taught him how to be a cowboy. Plus, he was the one who helped Liam moved here. I think Liam feels abandoned."

But I feel abandoned too, thought Vera. Her husband had barely spoken a word to her since his uncle's death. He would go out before breakfast and come back well after sunset. Vera had been occupying a lonely house where Henry died in.

Her heart dropped when she remembered that strange glossy look he gave her. She wished she hadn't been so quick to run away. At least then she would've had a better memory of his last moments. What she wouldn't give to hear her nickname from his lips again.

"Are you going to be okay?" Mary asked.

Vera wasn't sure. She wanted to ask her friend for help. But what could little old Mary do?

The Russian woman nodded. She didn't trust her voice to sound convincing enough. Mary patted her shoulder with a reassuring smile.

"It will be okay. He's in a better place."

Vera wished she had never spoken to Mary. She and Liam had to endure more people telling them that Henry "was in a better place" before they were finally allowed to go home.

As soon as they entered the house, Liam headed for the bedroom.

"Liam..." Vera trailed off. She was unsure how to proceed.

Her husband paused for a second, but didn't stop completely. He didn't look in her direction. And he didn't say a word. His newly gruff nature frightened Vera. This was not the man she married. It felt like she had a stranger in the house.

She wanted to tell him this. She wanted to plead with him to be strong for her just like she would try to be strong for him. But the words refused to come. He just stared right through her for so long it made her scared. Slowly, he turned back and walked away. Vera realized that she was all alone.

The next morning was when it started to fall apart.

"Liam?" she called while cleaning the dishes, "What are those hens making so much noise about? Can you check on them?"

No response. She dropped the plate on the counter and went to the other room. Liam sat in silence, polishing his rifle. She licked her lips nervously.

"Liam?"

He didn't say anything. Didn't even look at her. If his hands weren't moving, she might've thought he had turned into a statue.

"Liam. Please check on the hens. I'll go tend to the crops, alright?" she smiled at her compromise. Her smile faltered when seconds ticked by with no response.

Husbands wanted happy wives. Well, wives wanted happy husbands. Or at least husbands that would speak to their wives. Vera couldn't stand to look at him right now. She stomped outside and headed straight for the chicken coop.

Feathers and eggs were everywhere. Liam was the one who cleaned up the chicken coop and fed the hens. Vera noticed that there was no trace of bird feed in the coop. The chickens hollered at her for food, a few pecking her skirt angrily.

She closed her eyes and sighed. The woman went to the tool shed in order to do the chores her husband was supposed to do this morning. She grabbed the large bag of feed, making sure to lift with her knees in order to support it. They kept a ton of it in stock. This was why it was usually up to Liam to do it. Vera wanted nothing more than to go back to cleaning. At least that was work she was used to.

But if no one fed the chickens, their farm wouldn't get eggs, which was its main source of income. She barely made it through the door when a brainless hen got right under her legs, causing her to trip. She yelped. Feed spilled all over her, and the chickens rushed at the food. She sobbed dryly. Here she was, covered in feed, dirt and chickens, while her husband remained worthless.

She threw one bird off her shoulder.

Weeks passed and her husband would barely lift a finger to help her work. Weeks passed and she did both his chores and hers, slept alone because Liam no longer slept, and stopped trying to force food down her husband's throat. Weeks passed and her husband had not said anything to her. Vera had taken up so much work that she could've very well called the farm hers by now.

She carried the heavy sack to the chicken coop. Again she nearly tripped over one of the stupid fowls. She looked at the building. It was so dirty, but she didn't have time to clean it and make food and tend to the crops and feed the animals and churned the butter and sew new clothes for the coming fall.....

She couldn't take it anymore. Rage blinded her to all reason. Before she could consider what she was about to do, Vera stormed back inside.

"You worthless man. I'm ashamed of you."

Liam stopped polishing his rifle. He just stared at her. Vera knew she was being unfair right now. But she was too angry to care. She felt all alone. Without her husband, the only reason she had left her country, she had no one to turn to. It was all too much, and Vera found herself taking all her frustrations out on him.

"Why did I marry you? I was wrong to think that this would work out. I should've stayed in Russia. Now I'm all alone with a man who won't do anything."

Her husband didn't get angry, but his brows creased in sadness. She prayed that was enough to snap him out of it. However, instead of getting off the chair and helping her out, the broken man quietly went back to polishing.

They didn't look at each other for the rest of the evening. That night Vera couldn't sleep. Her dream life had become a nightmare. Every inch of her bones screamed in pain from all the hard labor she endured. And yet now that she had a chance to rest, she couldn't.

Giving up, the Russian went into the living room. Her husband sat snoozing on the chair with his gun in his hands. Vera realized that it was the first time in a long while that she had seen anything except distraught on his face. He almost looked....peaceful.

Vera shook her head. She looked at the chair he had so carefully made her and remembered what he said. He didn't even know how big she was before they decided to get married. Hadn't that been a warning in of itself? They didn't know each other before rushing into marriage. Otherwise she would've known that this would happen after Henry's death.

Letters hadn't been enough, surely.

Vera contemplated what to do now. Could she just leave? Just up and....leave? After all, Liam had obviously decided that she was no longer his priority. And it had been weeks of the same thing over and over again. She couldn't deal with this forever.

Vera sobbed. Maybe it would be better this way. Maybe she could go to Mary's house and ask to stay until she found a way back to Russia. This had all been a terrible mistake.....

She looked at Liam's sleeping face with her heart longing to love him. She refused to listen to it. Look where it got her so far.

Her mind was made up. She would be gone by the time that Liam awoke. Vera went into the barn and saddled the old colt that they had. She made a mental note to figure out a way to give him back to Liam later. The colt looked annoyed that she would make him work this late. She struggled to get on herself since she was so small, but still managed.

She set the horse in motion, dashing off into the night sky with nothing but the full moon as her light. She trusted her memory of the roads because it was so dark. The horse stepped on something wooden, informing her that they just arrived on the bridge.

She stopped. Someone was right in front of her, blocking her path. All she could tell was the manly silhouette. He grabbed onto her horse. She screamed.

"Let go!" she ordered.

"Is that you, Vera?"

The woman's heart continued to drum inside her chest.

"Orwell?" she gasped. She tried not to show her fear. God had not answered her prayers to get rid of this demon. And now it looked as if he had come to seek its vengeance on her.

"Calm down. I just want to talk to you."

"Let go."

She ushered for her horse to get out of there. But the colt remained motionless, almost as if entranced by this man in front of it. The man held up a lantern, revealing his face. Fear took control over everything else.

"I know what you are. Let me go!" she said.

"Please. I want to talk to you about your husband."

"What business is that of yours?"

Then, to her shock, the man let go of the horse. He backed away, but still stood right in the middle of the bridge. He held his arms out like a martyr preparing for his sacrifice.

"If you don't want to talk, I will let you leave. But keep in mind what you're about to do. I will not force you to stay and listen to me, but God is watching."

He spoke with sincerity, and with such adoration when he said God's name that it made Vera pause. Demons feared the Lord so much that they dared not speak His name. So how could he say it with such ease?

Vera got off the horse and slowly approached him. Logic told her to run far away. But something kept her feet moving forward. Maybe it was hope that he could tell her something she needed to hear.

"What is it?" she asked after a long silence.

Orwell's shoulders relaxed.

"I believe fate brought us together. Vera, I want to tell you that you can't leave your husband."

Vera didn't question how he knew what she was doing. Even if she decided he wasn't a demon after all, she still had a feeling that he was inhuman in some way.

He waited for her to respond. She just stood in silence, so he continued.

"Your husband isn't the strongest man alive. And that's why he needs you."

Vera shrank away at the responsibility she had been supplied with. Orwell noted her reluctance with a patient smile.

"He needs you to be his wife."

"You don't understand," she pouted like she was a child. She knew she was being unreasonable. But once again, she was too distraught to care.

"Then tell me until I do understand."

They were words of kindness, not mocking in the slightest. The man continued to hold the lantern up to his head so that she might see the sincerity on his face. She inhaled sharply.

"I'm in love with him...."

"....but?"

"I....I don't know what to do. He's throwing all of his problems on me."

"He's your husband. His problems are now your problems."

"But he's not the man he once was. Am I being cruel? I know his uncle died, but I've lost family too. Why do I have to be strong enough to keep us both together, while he does nothing?"

Right after she said it, she knew how selfish that was. The woman held her breath. She suddenly felt like God was glaring down at her in disappointment.

Orwell took his time coming toward her. He held the lantern on her face, taking in her expression.

His eyes were kind, "Your problems are his too. Tell me. If you love him, why are you running away?"

"....I don't know."

"Is it because you love him that you're leaving? Is it because you're tired of seeing him suffer?"

Shocked, Vera stared in awe at the man in front her. It was as if Orwell read her mind and put them into better words than she could voice herself. She had expected him to be angry with her for trying to leave. Instead he just stared at her with the upmost patience.

Could he be an angel of God?

The woman looked at him again, trying to see if there was some holy light circling around him. But his human disguise was flawless.

"You can still make the right choice. Turn back and go to him. You are one half of your husband's flesh. Without that half he will surely die."

Vera froze up. She hadn't thought about the scripture in that way. She hadn't considered how much Liam needed her. She figured that if she left, Liam would find a way to support himself again.

Had she been wrong?

The woman sobbed as guilt stung her chest. It felt like bees were digging their stingers inside her heart. She barely registered that Orwell had pulled her in for a hug.

"I don't know if I can go back," she admitted.

"Look inside yourself, just like you did when you came to this country. You're a girl who goes with her feelings. It's just that at this point in time, your feelings almost led you astray."

She looked at him with tears falling down her face.

He continued, "You know what the right thing is. God is telling you. I know you love Liam too, so your heart agrees with what God says. So what is telling you to run?"

She paused for a moment, thinking, "Fear."

"Get rid of that fear. God doesn't give anyone a spirit of fear, but of love and self-control."

This man knew his scriptures. He spoke about God like He was the one who personally assigned him this task. Vera looked him in the eye, wondering if it was really true. Did God send one of His angels to stop her?

She decided it must be true.

"Okay. Can you walk me back?"

Liam looked pleased, "Sure."

The minute they arrived at the farm, her husband came toward her. In the lantern light he looked in near hysterics. A flash of relief shone through his eyes, then he glanced at Orwell in suspicion.

"What happened? Where have you guys been, Bepa?" his voice wasn't accusing. But it did sound concern. Such worry touched her heart, making her more ashamed of her actions than ever. Orwell spoke up before she had the chance.

"You were asleep and we were afraid to wake you. I'm afraid I'm responsible for your little scare. I knocked on the door and your wife answered. I needed to borrow a horse to town."

"This late at night?" Liam exclaimed.

"It was an emergency. My own horse gone into labor and we needed to get supplies for a safe delivery. We just finish laying mother and baby to rest, and we're with you now."

Liam suddenly looked guilty.

"You're working at night too?" he sounded distraught, as if he just realized the weight he put on her shoulders.

Vera opened her mouth to say none of it was true. But Orwell looked at her. A flash of insight went through her mine when she looked him in the eye. Liam couldn't take the truth right now.

Liam pulled her into a tight embrace.

"I'm sorry. I should've tried harder. I should've remembered that you lost people too. When I woke up and saw you gone....I snapped out of it. I'm sorry, Bepa. It's just that....Henry was my father."

Tears stung Vera's eyes. She could understand the feeling of losing a parent. She returned the hug, promising herself to never make a repeat of this mistake again.

"I loved him too. But let me grieve with you. Don't push me away anymore."

He leaned his head into hers.

"I promise, Bepa," they kissed. Neither noticed the angel kindly leading the old colt back to the barn for a well-deserved rest. He smiled at the crops that he knew would bear the best fruit in town. God was good.

A COWBOY TO THE RESCUE

JOSIE DONOVAN

Chapter 1

California 1850

Annabelle Smith tiptoed to the door and placed her ear against it. A conversation floated to her. A conversation that made the hair on the back of her neck prickle.

"She was married before coming here," Mrs. Miller said.

"Well, the paying fools won't know. Half of them couldn't tell a maiden from a well-seasoned salon girl once in their cups."

Bile rose in her as her hand flew to her mouth. She should have known not to trust Miss Miller with her sweet offer of room and board at the orphanage. Should have known something was not right by the weary looks of the young girls she met or how they started disappearing. She needed to flee and she needed to flee soon.

She tiptoed back from the door and pushed a stray lock of her hair from her face. It had come loose from her chignon like it usually did.

"I will go and collect her," Mrs. Miller's said.

Annabelle gasped and stumbled back. She fell against the wall. They wanted to take her now. The door flew open, and a big burly man stepped out. A snarl accented the thick black and gray beard that covered his face and matched his sinister black eyes.

"I see our bounty has already come to us," he said.

Annabelle tipped her nose in their air like the plantation mistress in her home state of N.C. "Sir, I believe you're mistaking. I already have plans."

A harsh chuckle escaped him. "Yes, you do. But not the...."

Annabelle yanked the candle off the wall sconce and tossed it at the burly man. Flames engulfed his jacket as a curse slipped from him.

Annabelle raced to the door and flung it open as the sounds of pounding footsteps followed her. Perhaps, she could get to the inn. To hide out in the stables and wait for the stagecoach. Yes, the stage coach.

She turned down a small alleyway, between the saloon and merchant store, her gaze catching on a wagon. She glanced over her shoulder as she fell back against the wall, and ducked behind a barrel hidden by the wagon. Feet pounded past her. A rustle sounded as if the men looked through the wagon. Hopefully, the darkness would hide the barrel. For once she was thankful for the lack of a full moon.

"She must have gone into the saloon."

The pounding of feet sounded again and soon drifted away as a door opened and closed. She closed her eyes and fell back against the wall. "Thank you, Jesus," she whispered.

Johnny always said the Lord helped his faithful. A familiar ache filled her as tears gathered in her eyes. She couldn't believe he was gone, taking all their hopes and dreams with him. She could still see the lanky blonde hair young man who had owned her heart since she was a child. He was the son of a local doctor and her a cotton plantation foreman offspring. If Johnny hadn't come here with gold lust in his eyes, he would have never caught cholera, and left her alone with only the memory of his sweet kisses. She brushed a tear from her face. Lord willing, she would never marry again. Never face such a loss. But even as she made such a vow, she wondered how could she keep it. A woman had so few options.

She took a deep breath and stood, looking at the saloon door. She'd best hurry.

"I was wondering how long, you'd be hiding there."

Annabelle spun around and took a step back.

A man stood before her in a black suit with wear around the edges and a somewhat crinkled top hat. He held a lantern up higher, and his face came into focus. Old man Phillips.

"Ever find that so-called Uncle of yours?" he asked.

Annabelle looked down at the loose dust-like dirt on the ground. She had meant Mr. Phillips when she arrived in Glory Town looking for Johnny's uncle, hoping he'd help her. But like everything else she hit a dead end. The uncle had died in a cattle stampede right before she arrived. At the time, Mr. Phillips had been traveling with several mail order brides and had offered to include her. Had he returned from taking the brides further in the territory? Part of her wondered if his offer still stood.

"No, sir I didn't." She shuffled her feet.

"I told you not to trust Mrs. Miller," he said.

A crash sounded behind her, as shouts filled the air. She spun around, and stared at the wall, as a brawl broke out in the saloon.

"Mrs., I know of someone still looking for a bride. He's a godly man, with two children. A farmer. Couldn't do worse in your situation."

Her hand snaked to the calico fabric over her chest. She squeezed as the pain pulsed through her. How could she betray Johnny and become another's man bride? He had barely been dead a month. But what else could she do?

She turned, and looked back at Mr.Phillips. A softness radiated in his eyes. Maybe somewhere in that greedy business man's heart, there was a gentleman. "How old?" Her voice sounded like a squeak.

"Not too much older than you? 27 I figure."

"Could I meet him first?" she whispered.

A smirk crossed Mr. Phillips' face. "Of course you can, my dear."

Annabelle's shoulders slumped. Something told her, she just ran from the devil to make a deal with one of his demons.

Chapter 2

Annabelle looked out the window of the stagecoach as it drove into the small makeshift town. Only a few brown buildings made of wood lined the small street. Not one stone building could be seen. Men walked down the street with slumped shoulders and wearing dusty clothes ripped as if defeat had already claimed them. Where were the women? Children?

She leaned back from the window as Mr. Phillips' snore floated to her. He had slept most of the trip. The coach came to a stop with a small jerk. Hopefully, this Mr. Johnson had received Mr. Phillips' telegram stating he had found a bride for him. And hopefully, he would be everything Mr. Phillips said he'd be.

Mr. Phillips' eyes slowly opened and he turned to her. "Looks like we have arrived."

Annabelle remained silent, as the driver opened the stagecoach door and offered her his hand. She took it, and gathered her skirts, stepping out. Heat penetrated all around her as the blaring sun made her squint her eyes. Would she ever be used to such a dry weather?

Mr. Phillips took her hand, slipping it in his arm. He then guided her to where a small inn stood next to a mercantile store. Just as they stepped into the inn, Annabelle turned and stiffened. At the end of the street, sat a lone rider on a horse - his image slightly blurred by the sun. A prickle crawled over her skin. Why did that man seem to be focused on them as if he sought them? She shook her head. There was no way that burly man could have tracked her to here. Besides, why would he? Weren't there quite a few girls at the orphanage? But most of those girls were young, too young to work in a saloon. No, this man was just staring at her because she was a woman in a town which seemed to have a shortage.

Mr. Phillips led her to a small dining area with only three tables. Small vases with withered flowers decorated the table. He pulled out a chair for her and motioned for her to sit. He then left as he walked to where an older woman stood. The woman bent her head to him as he whispered something to them. What could they be talking about?

"Yes, he received the telegram, and should be here soon," the woman said just a little louder, quite possibly so Annabelle could hear.

Annabelle turned back to the table and folded her hands on it. Hopefully, Johnny couldn't see her from heaven. She imagined if he could he would feel such hurt. But then again, hadn't the Lord promised to wipe all their tears away in heaven?

The door to the small inn opened and clicked shut. She looked over her shoulder, her mouth slightly opening. A tall man with dark hair that swept over his forehead and curled at the nape of his neck swiped off his hat. His broad shoulders spoke of strength while his light blue eyes contained a softness that slightly contrasted with the roughness of his afternoon shadow. A small warmth spread through her. He was handsome like the men she read about in penny books.

He looked around and his gaze settled on Mr. Phillips.

Mr. Phillips walked to the man, holding out his hand. "Mr. Johnson, I didn't expect you so soon."

Mr. Johnson. He couldn't be the man, Mr. Phillips had in mind for her. He was too.... too grand. Annabelle reached up and patted the side of her head, hoping every strand of her mousy brown hair was in place. What was she doing? She yanked her hand down. How could she be wanting for another man to find her beautiful? Hadn't her love for Johnny been true?

Mr. Phillips walked towards her and placed a hand on her arm.

The man turned towards her, and narrowed his eyes, his gaze running over her. She wanted to slink behind Mr. Phillips and hide away. Apparently, she wasn't what he expected.

A sigh escaped Mr. Johnson as he shook his head.

"May I introduce you to the lovely, Mrs. Annabelle Smith. As I told you, she has experience with children and running a household."

Experience with children. Running a household. Unless Mr. Phillips counted how she cooked meals for Johnny over an open fire and tried to keep their thin tent neat running a household, she had no such experience.

Mr. Johnson nodded. "It's a pleasure to meet you."

"Shall we conclude our business? The pastor is waiting in the kitchen for us."

Mr. Johnson looked at Mr. Phillips, "I wish to speak to her alone if you don't mind. I promise to be a gentleman."

Mr. Phillips worked his jaw, before nodding and stepping away towards the kitchen.

Mr. Johnson looked at the closed door before he took her arm and led her further into the kitchen.

He then stopped and stepped in front of her, squeezing his felt hat. She looked at him, getting caught by his light blue eyes. How could a man have such pretty eyes? It was just not possible.

"Mrs. I must ask you something."

"What is that, sir?" she asked, a small tremble filled her voice.

"I must know if you willingly consenting to this. You appear so young."

Her mouth slightly parted. Kindness seemed to radiate from him.

"If you're being forced into this, I promise to help you even if you don't marry me. But I can't be apart of any underhandings. So please speak the truth."

He worried about her well being. What kind of man was Mr. Johnson? Perhaps he was one she could trust. And trust was important to her.

The opening of the door echoed in the background but she paid no mind to it.

"I am willingly consenting to this," she said, though an ache filled her, slicing at her heart.

"Well, hello again Mrs. Smith."

A gasp flew from her. She spun around, stumbling back against a firm chest. The burly man stood before her, with a smirk on his face. How had he found her?

"Who are you?" Mr. Johnson shouted over her shoulder. He pushed her behind him and clenched the gun on his holster.

"Just picking up my daughter," he said.

Annabelle clenched Mr. Johnson's arms as he glanced at her with raised brows. Tears rushed down her face as she buried her head into his back. Please, Lord, please help her.

"Your daughter?" Mr. Johnson asked. "She seems quite afraid of you."

"Aren't they always," he said as a hand gripped her. "I'd be collecting her now."

A swat sounded as the hand flew from her.

"Now...."

"Mrs. Smith, who is this man to you?"

A cry escaped from her.

"He isn't her father and I can vouch for that. Just a roughneck trying to force her into a saloon."

She glanced up noticing Mr. Phillips standing by the kitchen door, a shotgun in his hand.

"A saloon?" Johnson shouted. "Sir, I reckon you better leave. A click sounded, She glanced up noticing, Mr. Johnson had pulled out his gun, his stance strong and firm.

The burly man let out a loud laugh as he shook his head. "This ain't over, girl. You'll be mine," he turned and walked out the door, slamming it shut.

Annabelle's knees gave out as she fell to the floor. Strong arms swept around her, clutching her, keeping her from smashing against the ground. She looked at the firm line of Mr. Johnson's full lips. He'd never marry her now. But she needed him to. She needed the protection of a man more than ever.

"He is gone," Mr. Johnson said. "Are you alright?"

She nodded, as he lowered her to a chair. A glass was shoved into her hands, as the elderly woman raised it to her lips. She took a sip, her lips puckering at the sour taste. Lemon water. At least it helped clear her head.

Mr. Johnson stepped in her line of vision, squeezing his hat with his large hands. "Is he the reason you wish to marry?"

"Now..." Mr. Phillips spoke.

Mr. Johnson jerked his hand up, cutting off Mr. Phillips. "I'd like the lady to respond."

Annabelle looked down at the water, slightly swishing the cup. What would he say, if she said yes? But she had a feeling if she said no, he'd see right through her. She swallowed hard and gazed into Mr. Johnson's eyes, hoping hers could plead her case. "Please,

Johnson, I'll be an excellent wife. I just need a home." A tear slipped down her cheek, landing on her hands.

Something in Mr. Johnson's face softened as he bent his head to the side. For a man of great strength, his emotions had a way of decorating him.

He turned to Mr. Phillips. "Is the preacher still in the kitchen?"

***

From the corner of her eye, Annabelle glanced at the man who was now her husband. Even sitting, his head reached a foot above hers. His wrinkled hat had been planted over his head, pushing his hair slightly over his brows. He clicked his tongue and flicked the reigns of the wagon, urging the mule on. The wagon rocked slightly and she fell hard against his shoulder.

He looked down at her, a slight smile crossing his face. "You are a wisp of a girl."

Annabelle straightened, and folded her hands in her lap. She had always been on the small size, making people often think she was a child despite her 20 years.

"How old are your children?" she asked.

A smile tugged at the corners of his lips. "I have a son, 10, and a daughter 5. They're quite adventurous, but you'll love them."

They were older than she expected. Would she be able to become part of this family? To take on the role of mother? Besides the few slave children she interacted with on the plantation, she had no experience with children. How would she mother Mr. Johnson's? Luke's. He had told her to start using his Christian name. She best remember that.

The wagon pulled around a curve, and a small cabin with a nearby barn filled her vision. A young boy who mirrored his father in build lowered his ax. Several split logs sat in a pile nearby a tree stump.

She had arrived at her new home. Hopefully, the Lord would help her become the mother these children needed.

The wagon stopped and then creaked as Luke stepped off the wagon. He reached for her hand helping her down, before picking up some dry goods in the back of the wagon.

She smiled as the young boy who held his sister's hand walked towards them. The girl was small with dark brown hair pulled into two pigtails. Freckles accented her chubby cheeks and bright blue eyes. Eyes like her father's.

"Mary, Alex, I'd like you to meet Ms. Annabelle. She is to be your new mother."

The boy narrowed his eyes, pushing his lips into a thin line, while the girl just buried her face into her brother's leg.

Inwardly, she cringed. That was probably not the best way to introduce her. She forced a smile on her face despite the fear trembling in her. "I'm looking forward to becoming acquainted with both of you," she said, adding a slight curtsy.

The boy just shook his head and turned to walk away.

"Alex, I expect you to be...."

"Oh, no." She spun, tapping Luke on the shoulder. "We must give them time."

Luke planted his hands on his hips and towered over her, as the children continued to retreat. "Mrs. Johnson," he said with an edge in his voice. "Lets work out one thing right now."

"Yes," she said, taking a step back.

"You will never correct me in front of the children again. Do you understand?"

Tears pricked the corners of her eyes. Yes, she understood. She just didn't feel the children must be forced to accept her. "It's just we need to give them time."

"Annabelle," he growled out. "Do you understand?"

Annabelle clenched the sides of her dress. She must not anger him, but part of her ached for the children. Clearly, the boy was not happy about having another mother foisted on him. But alas, she couldn't anger her new husband especially since he had married her under such a precarious situation. She nodded.

"I'm glad we've come to an understanding." He adjusted the package in his arms. "Now run on in, while I settle the mule."

Annabelle turned and with slow steps walked to the cabin. Once at the door, she reached for the rope handle and pulled the door open, stepping in, glancing around. A small table with benches sat in the middle. Behind it was a black cast iron stove. There were two side doors on either side of the kitchen, hopefully leading to other rooms. For a farmer, Luke was doing quite well for himself. But then again, she knew farmers charged quite a penny for their fresh produce. The influx of men chasing after elusive gold had inflated the prices.

Annabelle ran her hand over the smooth table, noticing a small line of dust. Several rags sat in a corner, and a crusty pot with what appeared to be leftover porridge lay in a wash bucket. Luke did need a wife. She walked to where one of the back rooms waited and listened as a slight melody floated to her. Apparently, the boy sang a lullaby, probably to his younger sister. What could she do to reach these children who apparently had no desire for a mother? But every child needed one. Maybe she could try to be gentle and loving to win their trust.

She turned at the sound of the door opening. Luke entered with a slab of dried venison in his hand. He held it up to her and motioned to the stove. Dread seeped through her. Being a plantation foreman's daughter had afforded her luxury. She had lived in a modest home with a cook and maid. What would Luke think if he knew, she could only cook over an open fire. She had no idea how to even start a stove. Perhaps, it would be like the open fire. She'd just need to start a fire underneath.

She walked towards the stove and picked up a cast iron pan, straining under its heavy weight. She knew she needed to add some lard. She reached for a canister and opened it, looking at a white powdery substance. They could afford sugar. How long had it been since she had tasted such a rich treat? Her hand itched to reach in and scoop up a handful, shoving it into her mouth. She glanced over her shoulder, noticing Luke studying her. She set the jar down and looked at several of the canisters lining the shelf over the stove.

"The Lard's in the cool house.."

She flinched. Yes, of course, it would be. She started walking towards one of the doors.

"I'll get it," he said.

She turned as he walked out the front door. Now why did he go outside? She shook her head and walked back to the stove. She bent, opening the small black door, covered in soot. A few pieces of wood sat next to it. She placed several in.

"You're going to burn the house down."

Her gaze snapped up. The boy Alex stood next to her.

"You only need one," he said.

She looked in the stove counting six logs. An ache penetrated her, as she closed her eyes. Tears gathered in them again, as she reached in and pulled out several of the logs, leaving just one. She never realized how spoiled she had been being a foreman's offspring. She always saw the plantation daughters as spoiled with their full wide bell shape dresses always sitting as slave children waved fans over them.

She looked around for some way to start the fire realizing she had no idea. She had always used rocks and dried grass, but now she saw no such devices. A tear slipped down her face.

"Do you even know how to use a stove?" the boy asked.

"Alex," Luke growled out.

The boy shook his head and opened a small box near the stove. He took out two small stones and clinked them together until a small spark started. Hope filled her, as he walked to his father taking the lard. He dropped a tablespoon in and set the clay pot down. He turned to her crossing his arms over his chest. "I told you pa, we needed no one else."

"Alex, go milk the stalls now," he father shouted.

The boy huffed and raced out of the small kitchen.

Annabelle sniffled. The young boy was right. She had no idea how to use a stove. This had all been a mistake. A selfish mistake. She surely should have tried some other way to take care of herself instead of deceiving this family.

A large hand touched her shoulder. She stilled, as Luke stepped in her line of vision. Warmth spread through her as he reached to her face, and wiped a tear away with his large thumb. Warmth spread through her, as she got lost in his light blue eyes. What kindness radiated from them.

"This all will take some getting used to. I just ask that you try," he said.

"I've only cooked on an open fire." A tear slipped over her lips.

His hand strayed from her cheek to her lips as he brushed the tear away. Something awakened in her. An intense longing. A longing that seemed to mirror what she saw in her new husband's eyes.

"I'll help you," he whispered before dropping his hands. He turned from her, a slight ruggedness in his breath.

What had just happened? Why did the air around them seem to be so charged? Her dearly departed Johnny had never made her feel such intense emotions. She watched as Luke cut the venison into small pieces dropping them into the pan. She walked to where a basket held a few onions and radishes. Grabbing them she walked to where a cutting board hung on the wall. She grabbed it and lay it on the table before beginning to cut the onions. Luke glanced at her over his shoulder, a slight smile on his face. Something fluttered in her. Something that made her hope, she'd be the wife this man needed.

Chapter 3

A smile flitted across Annabelle's face as she walked towards the well, swaying the bucket in her hands. A small patter of feet sounded behind her. She turned and looked at Luke's daughter standing with her hands over her face. The dear child truly believed if she held her hands over her face, Annabelle wouldn't know she followed her everywhere. She turned back around and walked towards the well. She stopped at its mouth and started cranking the handle to lower the bucket. She glanced up and in the distance spotted, Luke and Alex working the wheat field. The mule dragged the yoke, turning up the rich soil. Streaks of orange and red raced over the skyline as the sun began to set. Soon the men would return from the field and as a family, they'd sit together for another meal. Thankfully, she had finally learned to use the stove.

Her first few weeks had been full of ups and downs, but she believed she was starting to settle in with the family. Her little shadow, Mary, was taken with her, and Luke seemed pleased with how, she had been began to manage the house. Only Alex remained aloof. But she couldn't blame him. The boy had memories of his mother, unlike Mary who had never known such a love, and obviously yearned for it. She had learned that the first Mrs. Johnson had died of bed fever shortly after Mary's birth. Every night, she prayed to her savior to give her wisdom on how to win over young Alex. He surely could. If He could die on a cross for the sins of the world, he'd help her find someway to soften a hurting boy's heart.

Mary peeked over the side of the well, holding a flower in her hand. Annabelle gave her a smile as she began to raise the bucket. The girl loved the sweet Chignon, she had tied her hair into last night. A fluttered filled her as she recalled the image of Luke sitting in his rocking chair, a smile on his face as she fixed his daughter's hair. Hopefully, she'd continue to please him because despite the recent loss of her first love, something in her seemed to be growing for the farmer she had married. Maybe soon, they'd share their first kiss.

Mary's eyes widened as the little girl stumbled back. What had frightened her? A hand gripped Annabelle yanking her back. A scream slipped from her lips. The scent of whisky assaulted her as a hot breath scathed her cheek.

"I told ya, you be mine,"

A click sounded in her ear. The burly man had found her.

"Now, you going to come with me nicely, or I'll shoot the little pixie. Ya hear."

Annabelle's gaze focused on the girl in front of her. Every part of her wanted to fight the madman who held her, but not at the cost of the sweet girl. She nodded and the man began to drag her backwards, her feet stumbling after him. Dear Lord, please protect her. Please.

Little Mary just stood frozen, her gaze planted on Annabelle. The man dragged her to a horse, and threw her over its black. The air fled from her as she landed on her stomach. The beast moved under her as the burly man swung up, sitting right behind her. His large hand gripped the back of her shirt, as he kicked the horse, sending it off in a trot. She turned to see Mary fleeing to the field. Tears rushed from her eyes. What could the she do? She couldn't just let this man take her from her family. She loved them. Needed them. Thoughts circulated through her mind.

Gunfire split the air. She glanced behind the galloping horse. Luke ran towards them, gun raised. He would never be able to save her. She just hoped, no prayed, that the Lord would see her through.

***

The man rode the horse through a thick forest, following a creek. Every now and then vines and branches would swipe at her face, but the nerves jittering through her, wouldn't let her feel pain. The horse slowed, and the man pulled on the reigns. She glanced up noticing a cave. At the mouth stood a man, she hadn't seen before holding a shotgun over his shoulder. He was tall and lanky, with dirt smearing his cheeks. A ripped jacket added to the vagabond look he adorned.

"She'd better be worth the trouble," the man said.

The burly man slipped off the horse, and grabbed her hips, pulling her off. Her feet crashed to the ground and she fell, landing hard on her backside. Pain ricocheted over every part of her.

"This isn't about worth. No girl gets away from me."

She should have known this was all about his pride. The burly man gripped her under the arms and yanked her to her feet. He pulled some twine from his pocket and wrapped it around her wrists, the wire slicing into her skin - small speckles of blood slipped through.

He then pulled her towards the opening of the cave, throwing her down on the ground. Her head slammed back against the wet moss covering the walls. Darkness nipped around the edges of her mind.

The burly man sat next to his thinner partner, and they began to pass a small tin amongst themselves. She licked her dry lips. Maybe if they imbibed too much she could sneak off. She did sit at the opening of the cave but darkness had completely fallen over the land. Could she survive out there alone? Would Luke come looking for her? With his vows, he had promised to protect her, but she imagined he must look after his children first.

She closed her eyes and leaned her head back. She needed a miracle, or by tomorrow she'd end up in a saloon, facing a nightmare.

"I told ya, we split, and no more." burly man yelled.

Her eyes flew open.

The thin man stood, planting his hands on his hips. His greasy blond hair made him look as though he hadn't bathed in weeks, probably months. "And I found you the buyer." His finger jabbed at her. "If you want to sell her, I best get a bigger cut."

A burly man jumped to his feet, yanking out the gun on his holster. "Don't you cross me, boy."

Was now her chance? If they got into a scuffle, they might not notice her slipping away. Annabelle slightly raised up, slipping closer to the opening as the men stared each down.

A thin man spit to the side. "You gonna shoot. You know, you can't outdraw me."

She glanced at the opening from the corner of her eye. She was mere inches from it.

"You might rethink that boy," burly man said.

Thin man yanked out his gun, firing.

Now was her chance. She jumped to her feet and raced into the darkness. Bullets sounded behind her richoteching off the walls. Maybe they were killing each other.

"Hey where you go," the burly man shouted.

She swallowed hard, as her feet stepped over rocks and tree roots. He at least had lived, and he knew she had fled.

A bullet blared past her, off to the right. She half ducked and then zigged zagged. Maybe if she didn't stay in a straight line, the movement and darkness would protect her from the madman's gun fire.

Her feet hit something hard. A cry escaped her as she fell forward, her face smashing into the ground. A throb covered her ankle. She tried to push up, but her right foot wouldn't move. Had she broken her foot? How would she get free? Images of her new family filled her mind.

She once again pushed up, wobbling on one foot. A hand gripped her. He had found her. Her gaze jerked, a small gasp escaping.

Burly man didn't stand before her. No, the man she now realized she loved did. How had he found her? He yanked his arms around her, crushing her into a tight hug. Kisses covered her head. "Thank you, Jesus," he said.

Crashing came through the trees. Luke pushed her behind him, his hand yanking out his gun. Burly man stepped into the small moonlight that illuminated the area, with a gun raised at them.

"Now isn't this sweet," he said, a snarl crossing his face. "A little reunion."

"Leave her be," Luke growled out.

"I've never been beaten and I'll never let a girl beat me, so you best hand her over before I play God."

A small ache filled her. She couldn't let Mary or Alex lose their father. She just couldn't. She reached a hand to Luke's cheek and rubbed the stubble growing there. "I can't let you be hurt. The children need you."

She turned to go to burly man, but Luke yanked her back into his arms. "And they need you," he said.

"She's a smart girl, You best listen to her."

A slow smirk crossed Luke's face. "Perhaps, you should look behind you."

"What?" The burly man spun as a shot rang out. He dropped to the ground, clutching a hand to his chest.

Young Alex stepped out from behind a tree, a shotgun in his hands. He held the gun up as Luke guided her over to the man. The burly man stared up towards the sky, with the life completely drained from his eyes. He was dead. And this was over.

Alex set the gun on the ground, and rushed towards her, throwing his arms around her waist. "You were going to sacrifice yourself for us."

Something warm swept into her heart as she pulled the boy closer. Yes, she would have because they were now her family. Thank you Lord, for providing a way to bridge the gap between her and Alex even if she almost lost her life.

"Let's get out of here. We need to get back to Mary." Luke said.

She nodded as Luke swept her in his arms. She looked back at the dead body. "We must inform the sheriff."

"In the morning."

In the moonlight they walked back to where the mule waited by the stream, licking up the water. Luke sat her on it and motioned for Alex to hop on. Luke helped the boy mount the animal.

Annabelle gripped the pommel, and looked down at Luke. "How did you find me?" she asked.

"I followed the horse's footprints into the woods and figured, if someone was going to hide anywhere, it'd be the caves. So just a lucky guess."

Or maybe the Lord had guided him and his son to right where she was. They rode in silence until they reached the cabin. Once there, Luke stopped. He helped Alex down and then told the boy to run on inside.

Once the door to the cabin closed, he reached for her hips, pulling her down. Her hands fell on his shoulders, as she leaned against him. He lay his forehead on hers, his hot breath coating her cheeks.

"Annabelle, I'm not a man of words, but I swear a part of me died when that man took you."

She gazed into his watery eyes and rubbed his chin with the back of her hand. "Thank you for coming for me. "

"I'll always come for you."

She leaned closer to his face, their lips mere inches apart. "You will?"

"Annabelle, I don't know how, but I'm falling for you."

"And I you."

Luke lowered his lips to hers, and a world of emotions exploded around her, as they shared such a sweet embrace. He pulled back from her and entranced her with his light blue eyes. "Then a family we shall be."

RODEO ROMANCE

JENNIFER CONLEY

The Wild West was a place for men to prove their supremacy. Only the strongest and most adaptable could survive the harsh terrain, the beasts, and the heartless people while coming out healthy and successful. Jack was determined to make a name for himself in the area. He grew up in the West, and he knew what it took to do it. He didn't have to look too far; his father, Butch, was one of the most known names in all of New Mexico. Butch was a well-known star in the up and coming rodeo circuit. He could round up cattle with his eyes closed, and he could trick ride with the best of them.

"When are you going to join the rodeo circuit? Now that your pops is retired, it's your turn."

Jack couldn't avoid the voices of the people in town. It had been that way his entire life. He grew up watching his dad perform, and he was easily as skilled as any other man his age in town. After all, he was trained by the best from a very young age. When Jack was only nine-years-old, he was a skilled horseback rider. As he got older, he continued to develop his skills. His father was extremely proud, but Jack secretly hated being under his microscope. He also hated being compared to him. Jack felt like his entire life had been planned for him since birth. He didn't hate roping and riding, but he didn't want to be forced into that career. He wanted to explore and see what else was out there for him. He couldn't really do that in New Mexico.

"Are you sure about this?" Butch asked. The father watched his son piling cargo onto his horse. Butch was tall, he had graying hair, and he had a tiny bit of dip stuck in his beard. Jack loved his father, and he didn't really want to leave; he had to leave.

"I think it's for the best," Jack said.

"Well, you're eighteen now. I can see why you want to go out and do things on your own."

"I'm glad you understand."

"Just don't forget what I've taught you along the way. The training will come in handy in a number of surprising ways."

"I couldn't forget it if I tried."

"Make sure that you and Willie stick together. It's much harder on the road when you're alone."

"He's my best friend, and we're going to do this together. Besides, he's the one who got us the job offer. I can't very well abandon him on the side of the road."

"Good. Just keep that in mind. And maybe try to find a nice lady while you're out on the road."

"Pa, I'm young and free. I don't want to be tied down yet."

"Just know that if you spend too much of your time with women with bad reputations, you might have a hard time finding a woman to settle down with later."

"OK, Pa."

"Don't just nod your head and say OK. You'll see that I am right."

"Well, I have to get going. I'll come back and visit when I am done with the season."

"I'll miss you."

"I'll miss you, too."

With that, Jack got onto his horse and headed to meet his best friend Willie and travel to California. They were going to work on a horse farm. Willie's older cousin needed help for the season, and Jack was quickly asked to come along because of his reputation. The work would be extremely easy for Jack. He would tend to the horses and relax in the sun during the day. To challenge himself during the days that he was bored, Jack imagined training the horses and chatting with Willie. He could also use the name to help teach Willie to be a better handler. And the best part was that he wouldn't be asked about his father or living up to his father's reputation. Even if people had heard of his father ,they wouldn't know that Jack was his son. He loved his father, but it was a relief to be alleviated from the immense pressure.

Jack rode down the road until he arrived at Willie's small farm. Willie was at the front of the small house waiting for Jack.

"Are you ready?" Jack asked excitedly.

"Of course, I am! Let's go do this!"

Willie and Jack quickly headed out on their journey to California. It would take them a couple of days, but they were determined to get to their destination as quickly as possible. Willie's cousin made it very clear that he needed the help as quickly as possible. Jack and Willie were going to arrive early and surprise their boss with the dedication and how quickly they could get a job done. If they did well, he might hire them for the next season. He might even pay them a little more!

"Come on! We need to go faster!" Jack called. Willie was lagging behind him a couple of yards, and Jack wanted him to learn to keep up with his pace. By the end of this trip, Willie would have amazing riding skills. He would need them, too, if they were going to work on a horse farm. Jack's father had given him great riding skills, and he gave him amazing leadership skills. If anyone could teach Willie, it was Jack.

The men sped through the night as fast as the horses could manage, stopping for water and food a couple of times throughout the day. Jack worked his horse hard, and he made her ride for as long as possible, but he also took good care of Pegasus. She was well fed, hydrated, and she was fit and strong.

Pegasus never wandered off on her own or misbehaved. She was not only well trained, but she loved Jack. She didn't want to leave his side unless they had to.

"She's the best-trained horse I've ever seen," Willie said. "I always knew that she was good, but this is remarkable." Pegasus meandered around the small river that they had stopped at to drink water.

"I've had her for just about six years. I've been training her since she was little. We have a bond."

"Yeah, you've had her for as long as I can remember. I hope I can be as good with the horses on the farm as you are."

"You'll be just fine. There will obviously be a couple of wild horses that don't want to be restrained. I'll show you how to handle those when we start working."

"I couldn't think of anyone else better to bring with me to do this. I know you don't like people comparing you to your dad, but it's great that he was able to teach you so much."

"I also worked really hard to achieve my skills."

"I'm sure that you did. But you have to admit that you had access to a much better trainer than most people."

"My father was a great teacher," Jack said, getting annoyed with the conversation.

"I'm surprised that you didn't want to be a part of the rodeo circuit. You could really make a name for yourself."

"You mean I could take my father's name and use it to help get myself in the rodeo. I'd rather become successful by myself. Besides, my father has had plenty of falls. He didn't quit by choice. He quit because his body couldn't handle it anymore. Luckily, he survived. Many men don't. What would happen if I got into a terrible accident?"

"You could get into an accident anywhere."

"I don't have to go looking for it, though. If I joined the rodeo, I would get hurt eventually. Let's just keep going forward to the horse farm."

They got back onto their horses and continued to ride. It took them days to get to their destination. They were running out of supplies by the time they arrived at the farm in California, and Jack couldn't be more relieved to be at their destination.

They found Willie's cousin, Larry, out in the farm tending to the horses. There were horses of all different sizes and all different colors. Some were mild mannered, and some were aggressive. Jack smiled surveying the acres of land that the horses had to explore. This is where they would grow up, play, eat, copulate, and develop their skills.

"Larry!" Willie shouted out to the man to get his attention. He rode over on his horse right away and greeted his cousin and Jack.

"Am I glad to see you! There's plenty of work to be done around here. The famous Jack, is it?"

"Yes, sir. Thank you for hiring me for the reason. I'm mighty good with horses, and we will be sure to help keep them well cared for, fed, and help with breeding."

"That's exactly what I need you for. I have to tend to the rest of the farm, and it's been impossible for me to manage since I lost my help. I've been working eighteen hour days the last couple of weeks, and I still can't get everything done," Larry said.

"Well, I suppose you want us to get started right away," Jack said.

"Not necessarily. I know you both must be tired and hungry after your trip. Why don't you go ahead and get some food from inside? My wife has some potatoes and ham. You can help yourselves before it gets cold. You can get to work after that."

Jack and Willie made their way inside to get some food before they started working. The food was the best thing that they had the entire trip. They both desperately wanted to fall asleep after riding as much as they did the last couple of days, but they knew that there was too much to be done.

They got out to the farm and started working diligently. They did whatever they could to help. They had to help clean up the waste that covered the pastures and store it for fertilizer in the area designated for growing food. They continued to also help clean some of the horses and feed them. Jack fell in love with each and every single horse that he came across. At one point, he took an especially lively horse for a quick ride around the pasture to bond with it. The horse was strong and determined. It tried to surprise Jack and scare him, but Jack was able to maintain control and never showed a single side of weakness. The horse finally relaxed and let Jack guide her closer to the stables.

"You don't need to show off what your daddy showed you quite yet!" Larry called out to Jack.

"Just bonding with these beautiful creatures. Establishing dominance."

"It was quite impressive. That is Lightning. We've never been able to tame him like that. You might really have some skills, young man."

"I like to think so."

"Well, I'm glad that you're a part of the team. Now, it's getting dark. We gotta start taking the horses into the stables for the night."

It took a long time to get the horses comfortably in the stables. Jack was glad that there was plenty of space for Pegasus. She also seemed relatively happy. Before bed, Jack had to put all of the supplies into the barn. He walked into the dark building with his hands full. As he tried to put things away in the unfamiliar barn in the dark, he could hear a distinct rustling.

"Hello?" he said. Was it a small animal? It sounded too big to be an animal. Could it be Willie trying to play a prank on him? That had to be it! "Willie, you get your ass out here before I start shooting!"

"Wait! Please! Don't!" a small feminine voice said. Then, a small girl came out from hiding.

"Hi. I'm Lily."

"What the hell are you doing here?" Jack asked.

"I'll explain. Just please don't shoot!"

"I'm not gonna shoot a girl. What are you doing here? Trying to steal? Are you here for a horse or some crops? Get out of the barn and into the light so I can see you."

Lily walked out of the barn slowly with her hands visible. She was young, too thin, and she had pretty blonde hair and blue eyes. Her clothes were dirty and tattered. She also had a prominent black eye.

"I was not here to steal anything. All I wanted to do was get some shelter for the night. You have to believe me," said the girl fighting tears.

"Why are you on the run? Did you steal from someone else? What did you do?"

"I didn't do anything I swear!"

"Then why do you find yourself hiding in a stranger's barn at night to protect yourself from the elements?"

"I had to leave my house. It was horrible. I can't explain it."

"Did your husband give you that black eye? You look a little young to be married already."

"I'm seventeen. Plenty of girls my age are married."

"So it was a husband then? Or a boyfriend? Did you run off with some dangerous cowboy only to wind up sorry?"

"It was my father!"

"Your father?"

"Yes! I've been trying to escape his grips for a long time now. I finally did it. I don't have anywhere to go now."

Jack looked at the poor girl with sympathy. She was clearly hungry and dirty. It wasn't his home to offer her food or any other help.

"Are you going to call the sheriff on me for trespassing?" she asked.

"I don't think that's necessary," Jack replied. "Wait one moment. I am going to get the owner of the farm."

"Please don't do that!"

"I'm not doing it to get you in trouble. I'm doing it for your own good. Maybe they can help. Just come with me."

Jack and Lily walked over to the house with Lily slightly behind Jack the entire time.

"Who do you have there, Jack? I didn't realize that you brought a stowaway with on our trip," said Willie.

"This here is Lily. I saw her wandering around outside. It looks like she could use some help."

"What are you doing around here alone, child?" Larry asked.

"What the hell happened to you? This girl needs some ice for her eye. She's also bone thin. We need to get her some food right away!" Larry's wife said, scrambling.

The entire family rushed to help the girl who was obviously in need. Jack smiled when he saw the girl in clean clothes eating a warm meal at the table with the family. She looked quite pretty all cleaned up, even with the black eye.

"You have to tell us exactly what happened to you," Jack said. "Why did your dad hit you?"

"And there's no need to lie. Tell us the truth, because we'll find out one way or another," said Larry.

"I have no reason to lie. My family is not a great family. My dad is Buck Clayton-"

"Buck Clayton is your father?" interjected Wille. "I can't imagine the hell that you've seen."

Everyone knew who Buck Clayton was. It was well known around the entire United States that Buck Clayton was an evil criminal who dipped his toe into just about every criminal activity available. He was an outlaw who robbed people and then moved to another state to avoid getting caught. There were numerous stories of his ruthless behavior, and it was hard to believe that all of them were made up.

"How do we know that you're not a cheat and a thief like your father? You were probably just trying to rob me," Larry said. "Get this girl out of my house."

"Oh, Larry. Watch your mouth. This poor child obviously needs help. I can't imagine what it would be like growing up with that beast as a father," said Larry's wife.

"I didn't see him much," Lily started to explain. "He was always out doing God knows what. I stayed with my ma. She met my pa at a brothel out here in California, but she left that life and became a simple seamstress when she got pregnant with me."

"How do you even know that Buck Clayton is your father?" Willie asked.

"They met at a brothel, but they traveled together for months before he had to abandon her because the sheriffs were on his trail. She found out she was pregnant just days before he ran off. I saw him again the other day. He actually came looking for me. I know that everyone says he's such a bad man, but I actually thought that maybe he'd be gentle and warm. I was actually happy to see him. I was very wrong, though. He ended up trying to hurt me and sell me to these men-" Lily started crying, but she did what she could to maintain her composure. "I got the black eye when I tried to fight him off. I was able to get away and run. To think. I could've been someone's slave right now. How could a father do that to a child?"

Larry's wife consoled Lily and helped wipe away her tears.

"Well, child. That is just plain unacceptable. We are going to help take care of you starting today."

"And how do you plan to do that, Linda?" Larry snapped.

"Well, we can give her a job. You have all these hands helping you out in the fields while I spend my days cooking and cleaning alone. I have chores, too, ya know!"

"Well, I guess I don't see the harm in that," Larry said. "But there are no second chances in this house, girl. The second you cause a problem, you are out. You will be paid in food and a cot to sleep in. You will get a very small stipend every day."

"Thank you so much!" Lily jumped up and faced Jack. "And thank you so much for making me come meet everyone. I can't thank you enough."

The next day, Jack woke up to the smell of breakfast filling the small house and the sound of Lily and Linda laughing in the kitchen.

"It sounds like you're getting settled in," Jack said to Lily.

"Well, it's easy when I have someone as amazing as Linda to keep me company."

"And it's easy to be good company when I have such a busy bee in my kitchen. She knows what she's doing in the kitchen, and she knows how to keep everything clean," Linda said. "You're going to make some husband very happy someday."

"And hopefully, I'll be a help to you for now," Lily smiled.

Jack was happy to see that Lily and Linda were getting along.

"Well, we have to head out to the fields. You ladies have a good day."

"It will be a great day. I might even find some time to sew!" Linda said happily.

Jack and Willie went out to the farms to work. The sun blasted down on Jack causing him to sweat from his forehead profusely. Luckily, Lily was sent out to the fields a couple of hours into the day with large canteens of water.

"Here," she said, handing one to Jack. "It's cold." Her smile was so sweet and sincere.

"Thank you," he said.

"I really do owe you another thank you," Lily said. "I can't believe how well this turned out for me. I promise that I will work hard and make Linda and Larry happy to have me on the team this season."

"And what do you plan to do after that?"

"Well, I think I'll have enough saved up to travel somewhere to get a job."

"Good luck," Jack said. "Well, I have to get back to work. You probably do too."

As Lily went to go give Larry and Willie their water, Jack noticed that he could make out her recently developed body in the clothes that Linda had let her borrow. He couldn't help but fantasize about Lily for the rest of the work day.

"Jack! Look alive!" Willie said riding up next to Jack. "You look like your mind is somewhere else. I knew that this would be easy for you, but you still have to pay attention."

"I always have my eyes open. I was watching what I was doing the whole time."

"Alright, buddy. Did you happen to look at Lily today? I wouldn't mind taking her out to pasture if you know what I mean."

"Don't be crass about the poor girl. It is true that she is very pretty, though."

"I seriously might see if I can take a walk with her later."

"What about Jessica back home? We're going back at some point."

"She never has to find out," Willie smiled.

Jack couldn't stay silent.

"Well, I think that I'm going to ask her to go for a walk tonight. I don't have anybody back home. You should let me do it," Jack said.

"I got you!" Willie laughed. "I didn't want to court Lily. I just wanted to get you to admit that you wanted to. It's hard not to see how you look at her."

"I suppose you want a thank you for that?" Jack asked. "Let's just get this work done."

Jack and Willie had plenty more work to do. It took them hours to get everything done.

"I'm heading in!" Willie screamed into the stables.

"I'm almost done here. I'm gonna brush Pegasus and a couple of the horses, and I'll be in," Jack told him.

Jack slowly brushed Pegasus who nudged him and neighed playfully. Her coat was a stunning white color that seemed brighter than the snow with large auburn patches scattered around her strong body. Her mane was thick and white. She looked like she could be a prize horse the way that Jack took care of her, and they both loved each other dearly.

"She's beautiful," Jack heard Lily say from behind him. She was carrying a small lamp for light. "I didn't mean to startle you, but I was told to come get you. It's getting late, and you haven't eaten anything since that little bit for lunch."

"It's hard for me to tear myself away from her. She's my favorite thing in this entire world.

"I absolutely love horses, too. I used to ride all of the time. I never had a horse that was all my own before, though."

"It's a lot of responsibility."

"I could take on the responsibility. I would be just as dedicated as you are with Pegasus."

"You used to ride? Do you want to go for a ride right now?"

"It's dark. And I'm not sure what Larry and Linda will think of that."

"I don't think that they'll mind. Pick whatever horse you want," Jack said.

They went out on their horses and seemingly galloped into the star-filled sky. Linda rode just as quickly as Jack did, and she had no problem following Jack through the rough terrain and small jumps. They rode around the property for a good thirty minutes before they went back to the stables.

"You do know how to ride," Jack said approvingly.

"It's always been a passion of mine."

"Well, we should probably get back in."

Lily stepped in front of him before Jack was able to leave the stable.

"You know," she said. "I offered to come and get you."

"Oh?"

"I wanted to be able to spend some time alone with you."

Lily's body kept getting closer to Jack's. She gently put her hand on his chest and looked up at him with her crystal blue eyes. Jack couldn't resist himself, and he kissed Lily long and hard in the stables.

Jack went to bed that night thinking of how he should react to Lily's advances. He couldn't get her sweet taste off of his lips, and he didn't want to. She tasted as sweet as her voice sounded. He found himself wishing that he could kiss her more, and he secretly wanted her in his bed.

When he saw her the next morning, he found himself unsure of what to say, so he went about breakfast quietly and sat as far away from her as possible.

"You two didn't get back in until after dark," Linda pointed out. "It took Lily over a half hour to get you!"

"I was brushing Pegasus, and we decided to go for a quick ride. Sorry if it took so long."

"No, no. Just be careful riding in the dark. What if the horse can't see something and you get hurt?"

"We were safe enough," Lily said. "And it was a lot of fun."

The days went on, and there were no other interactions between Jack and Lily. In fact, Jack made a point to try to avoid her. He kept busy with Willie and Larry. When in the house, he made sure that plenty of people were around. Jack wanted to repress his feelings as much as possible, but it was difficult. As often as Jack tried to prevent them from being alone together, Lily seemed to make it her mission to find alone time with him. It took a couple of days, but she finally found him in the stable again after a day of working.

"Are you avoiding me?" Lily asked bluntly.

"I'm not avoiding you," Jack said. "I just don't think that starting a relationship right now would be the best thing."

"Why?" Lily demanded. "Is it because I'm not pretty enough? Is it because of my father? I'm not going to be my father, and there's nothing to be afraid of."

Lily's black eyes had dissipated, but Jack could see the pained expression on her face.

"It's not because you're not pretty. You're beautiful. And it's definitely not because of your father."

"Oh, sure. You say that. I've heard people say that before, too. You don't want to look like a chicken, but you're afraid. I'm sick of people always associating me with my damned father!"

Jack thought back to all of the times that people asked him when he was going to join the rodeo like his father. He also thought of all of the times that people called him his father's name by mistake. He left to create his own identity. At least his father was a respected member of the rodeo, though. He couldn't imagine being associated with the scrupulous Buck Clayton.

"It has nothing to do with your father," Jack said softly caressing the young girl's face. "I promise."

"Then what is it? Because I'm poor? Because you don't want a wife?"

"To be honest with you, I didn't want a wife before I met you. I never thought that I could meet somebody so pretty and strong. And you know how to cook and take care of a house," Jack said. "You're the perfect girl."

"I don't understand."

"I've just never done this before. It's different for me."

"You've never been with a woman before?"

"I've been around before. I've never found a girl that I considered courting."

"Well, don't be afraid! You're strong, handsome,and you rescued me when I was in trouble. My life changed in a great way when I met you. I don't want to go back to my life before you."

She was so beautiful and adoring. Jack couldn't resist his feeling for much longer. He pulled her in for a passionate kiss, watching her breasts heave in her dress. Her kisses tasted like citrus, and he continued to kiss her. Short and sweet kisses as well as long, passionate kisses with his tongue. He felt a strong desire for Lily, and he wanted nothing more than to spend the entire night in the stables with her dress on the piles of hay. He stopped at kissing, though .Pulling back a bit to pause their passion before it got too intense.

"Would you like to go for a walk around the property?" he asked.

"Absolutely."

They walked side by side through the clear pastures in silence for minutes that seemed to be an eternity. Jack casually slid her hand into his own, and she smiled up at him.

"You do look quite stunning under the glow of the moon and the stars," Jack told her.

"Why thank you. I thought I looked quite unattractive when you first saw me. I was worried that you wouldn't be able to get past that first impression."

"I didn't think that you were ugly at all. I thought that you were beautiful, but you were in need of help."

"You were right. I did need help. And you were there for me," Lily smiled.

"I couldn't leave a girl in that situation. You're tough, though. You got to work right away and started taking care of yourself. Some other people might not have had that strength. It's quite admirable. And I'm sorry about your father. No one deserves that."

"This may not make sense to you, but somehow the way he tried to kidnap me didn't hurt me nearly as badly as the way people look at me when they know who my father is. I tell most people that I don't know who my father is. That makes things a lot easier."

"I actually do understand that. My father is famous in New Mexico. He's been in the rodeo for my entire life up until recently. People are constantly asking me when I"m going to join the rodeo or telling me how much better my dad was when he was my age."

"That's really not so bad," Lily giggled. "I'd rather have your dad than my dad."

"Fair enough."

They spent the night walking around the property and talking until they could start to see the sun peeking up from the ground.

"We need to get at least an hour of sleep," Jack said.

"Do we have time for one more kiss?"

"Of course," Jack said. He kissed her in the middle of the meadow with the sun slowly starting to rise.

Jack and Lily refused to hide their affection going forward. When they were abruptly confronted by Larry, Linda, and Willie, they didn't lie.

"We were walking and talking together all night," Jack said. "I was lucky to have such an attractive companion with me."

"And I was lucky to have such a strong and handsome man to accompany me."

"Well, look at you two being all lovey-dovey," Willie laughed.

Their honesty allowed Jack and Lily to spend more time alone together. They enjoyed private walks or horseback rides almost every night. As the season started coming to an end, there were a lot of unanswered questions that they would have to address.

"Where are you planning to find a job after this?" Jack asked.

"'I'm not really sure. I guess I figured that I would go back home."

"You can't do that. What if your father comes back to find you?"

"Well, what about my mother?"

"She shouldn't stay there either!"

"And what are you suggesting I do?" Lily asked.

"Why don't you consider coming back to New Mexico with me and Willie?"

"New Mexico is so far away on a horse! And I'm not sure your father will like me. He probably expects you to join the rodeo and find the prettiest girl around."

"I already have," Jack told Lily.

"I'm juts nervous. And what if my father finds me in New Mexico?"

"Then I will protect you from him. No one is going to take my woman away from me!" Jack said. "Don't worry about anything."

The next day, Jack had to go to town for Larry. He was the fastest on a horse, and he could make the trip in the shortest amount of time. He was going for simple supplies, but they were necessary to complete work and cook dinner. The nearest town was only about fifteen miles away, so the ride was only about two hours long. The town was charming. It had a bank, saloon, general store, tailor, and plenty of other little shops. People walked down the roads in clothes that were nice but not their Sunday best. There was also a beautiful jewelry store in town that Jack decided to visit.

When Jack got back to the farm, the day was almost over. He went in the house and dropped off the food that he picked up from town.

"Finally! Now we can have a proper dinner tonight," Linda said. "You're going to have to go back out and give the men their supplies. We'll get supper ready."

Jack went out to help finish up the last of the chores. He didn't even mind getting the horses back into the stables and caring for them anyway.

At supper, everyone laughed and joked until it came to a question of what everyone was going to do once the season was over. The season was only going to last for two more weeks.

"Now that you two are becoming chummy, are you thinking of heading back to New Mexico together?" asked Larry.

"We've talked about it slightly, but we really haven't completely decided," Lily said. "I guess we have the next two weeks to figure it out."

"I think that's a hint," Linda laughed.

"You think?" Jack replied. "We will see what happens.

At that moment a large force knocked down the front door of the small house. Everyone at the kitchen table jumped, shocked by the surprise. On the other side of the busted door stood a large man. He was both tall and sturdy, and he had a huge scar across his forehead. His teeth looked black from tobacco. The pistol in his hand grabbed the attention of everyone the moment they saw it.

"Give me my daughter," the man growled. "She forced me to lose out on a pretty expensive deal recently. I'd like to make that deal happen."

Lily froze at the table in fear. It became very clear that the family was face to face with the infamous Buck Clayton himself. Buck aimed the pistol at his daughter. Jack needed to protect her, but if he made too swift of a move it could cause Buck to shoot Lily. Throughout the entire situation, no one at the dinner table spoke a word.

"You heard me, Lily! Get up! Once you come with me, I will leave these nice people alone."

Lily's frightened face glanced over at Jack not sure of what to do. He slightly nodded to her, and she slowly started getting up from the chair.

"You caused me a lot of problems, little girl. You thought the black eye was bad? That won't compare to the whopping you're about to get from me now. Did you think I wouldn't be able to find you?"

Lily slowly walked toward her criminal father with her head down. Jack could see that the gun was still pointed at her. When Lily was taking too long, Buck leaned up to grab her by the wrist. Jack couldn't wait anymore, and he jumped up, grabbed the pistol from his holster, and shot at Buck before he had a chance to know what had happened. Both Lily and Buck fell to the floor, but luckily Lily was able to get back up.

"Fetch the sheriff!" Jack screamed as he tied up the dying man on the ground. "If he's not dead, he will at least go to jail."

Willie immediately ran out of the house to find someone to appropriately take the hardened criminal away.

"You know, there may even be a hefty reward for catching Buck Clayton," Larry said.

"Well, we'll all share it then. But until the sheriff gets here, I have one very important question to ask Lily."

With Buck tied up and subdued on the ground and broken pieces of wood from the door scattered about, Jack got down on one knee and pulled a small ring box out from his pocket.

"Lily, will you marry me?"

TO TRUST AGAIN

NATASHA GROVER

To trust again...

When Annie's long-time boyfriend decides that the Amish way was no longer his way, she is left shattered, but worst of all single. She struggles to overcome rejection and prays for God to help her, but all she gets in return is silence. Barren and a spinster, she had lost all hope of finding love. But through revelation during a Sunday service, she discovers that there is hope, and that is when everything changes.

When Seth and his daughter Mary arrive in town, everything changes. A chance meeting with a beautiful woman who adores his daughter was nothing but the grand design of God.

God works in mysterious ways, and this is exactly what happens when two souls are meant for each other.

Chapter 1

Annie looked down at the small keepsake box Abel gave her last Christmas. She never thought she would feel this way, so deserted and lost. Abel was the only man she ever cared for and now he was gone, out of her life and out of her world, but still so very present in her mind. She couldn't believe it when he came to her just a month ago to tell her he was leaving for good. Everything seemed so perfect, she was happy; she thought he was happy and although he often told her how he would have liked to be able to study science instead of erecting barns and toil in the fields, she never expected him to follow that farfetched dream of his. After all, his father was the Bishop of Lititz and he knew the consequences of his actions, yet here she was staring eternity in its face with no hope to marry one day. *How could God have allowed this to happen,* she thought as tears welled up in her eyes, surely He would not have allowed such a worldly passion to overcome Abel and allow his servant and son to run into a world where evil is so rife.

"Annie, it's time to let it go," Anke said as she came to stand next to her.

"Not now Anke," Annie mumbled, wiping the tears from her cheeks.

"You've been a walking corpse since he left, you hardly eat and all you do is sit here and sulk, sooner or later the pain will go away, but only if you let it go."

"It's easy for you to say, you have everything," she blurted out and stormed into the house to find the solitude of her room.

Anke was her younger sister, what did she know of heartbreak? It wasn't as if she could simply turn off a switch and stop feeling so terrible. She was married, she had everything Annie ever wanted, she had a loving husband a child and her life was perfect. Anke knew better than to envy her sister, but her emotions were all over the place and right now not in the best of places either. If only she could turn back time and try harder to convince Abel to stay. But now that she had time to think things over it became more and more evident why Abel never proposed to marry her. He never intended to stay, and after Bishop King's passing, there was nothing to stop him from pursuing his dream. If he loved her like he so often said, then why did he break her heart? He didn't even ask her to join him, not that she would have, but if he had asked her then she would have been certain that he did in fact see a future with her, but then it would have been her choice to stay. But instead he went on his own, because he wanted to leave everything behind, including her.

She slammed the door to her room shut and pressed her back up against it, this raging sea of anger was suffocating her in ways unimaginable. She was angry with Abel, with Anke and even with her youngest sister Mabel. Convicted by the thought of being angry even with God, she tossed the keepsake box aside and fell to her knees.

"Forgive me Father; I'm a simple person with a broken heart. Please take away this pain and heartache," she prayed as tears streamed down her face, "Please help me to understand why everything is going wrong in my life. Have I not been a loyal servant?"

She waited expectantly for an answer or for the pain to miraculously disappear, but the silence was like a poison that seeped into her blood and paralyzed her. The emptiness she felt was overwhelming and cruel, "Why have Thou forsaken me?" she cried. It felt as if God had turned his back on her, even though she had no idea why. She searched the recesses of her mind, trying to make sense of it all, trying to remember any sins she may not have asked forgiveness for, but nothing came to mind. Rejected by her one true love and by God, she curled up on the floor and wept.

Chapter 2

Two days have passed, since her melt down in front of her sister, and thankfully Anke did not poke at her again, but the emptiness was far from gone. Numb she sat against the wall in Bishop Troyer's house with everyone else occupying the space for the Sunday Service. She felt almost alienated and the looks of sympathy she got from her peers didn't help her mood either, she was an utter disgrace, not to mention humiliating. All the other women her age was settled down with their own families. And at the age of twenty-nine she had nothing but broken dreams strewn in the wake of a failed relationship.

Caught up in her own thoughts she paid little attention to the service, until Bishop Troyer clapped his hands together and exclaimed loud enough for her to pay attention, "Trust in the Lord with all your heart and lean not on your own understanding; in all your ways submit to him, and he will make your paths straight."

That was her moment of realisation, all this time she had been trying to make sense of it all with her own understanding. And she was too emotional to thing rational, she still had a lot of questions as to why God had taken Abel from her when she was so sure they were promised to one day marry, but if she was going to get through all of this she was going to have to put her trust in God.

After the service she felt less burdened, almost as if a weight had been lifted, the longing was still there but it was lighter than before and instead of going home she took a walk down the small path that led to the a nearby brook. A time for reflection was nigh and by the grace of the Father, she could finally be free. She sat down in grass near the stream and closed her eyes, raising her face to the sun and soaking in it warmth. The spinning chaos that had altered her world over the past month or so was suddenly replaced by hope and for that she was grateful for.

"Daed!" a little voice called not far from where Annie was sitting and she quickly opened her eyes and looked up stream, and then she saw the little girl in her blue dress skipping towards her, and not far behind her, her father or so she would assume.

"Hello," the little girl said as she reached her, "why are you sitting here?"

"Mary, where are your manners?" her father reprimanded when he reached her, "I'm so sorry, she gets out of hand quite quickly," he apologised and Annie simply smiled.

"It's quite alright, I was just enjoying the fresh air," she said to the little girl, "My name is Annie," she smiled and extended her hand to the little girl, who suddenly shyly hid behind her father.

"She's embarrassed now," he chuckled and pulled her out from behind his legs, "Say hello to Annie."

"Hello Annie," the little girl, who couldn't have been older than five or six years greeted, with her thumb stuck in her mouth and her toes pointed to each other.

Annie did not recognize them, although their community was sizable and she didn't know a few people by name, she would surely have remembered the faces. And as far as she can recall she hadn't seen the little girl at the local school where she often helps out as a teacher's aid, but then she may not be six yet.

"I'm Seth," he said and tipped his hat, "Mary likes to come here whenever we come to Lititz."

So they were not from around here, she realized raising her hand to cover the bright sunlight streaming down from above, "Where are you from?"

"Rothsville, we came to attend the church service at least once a year in honour of my belated wife."

Annie's heart cramped in her chest, as she realized he was widowed, yet his tone of voice sounded uplifting as if he had made peace with his loss.

"Mamm died of cancer," little Mary piped up.

She had a maturity level Annie hadn't seen in a child for a long time, and realized that it may be because of her loss.

"My condolences to you," she cleared her throat, "It must be a difficult time for you."

"It's been a year and some months now, Meryl was from here originally, and I promised her that I will bring Mary here, she always liked it here by the stream."

"Why do you come here?" Mary asked again and this time Annie pushed herself up to on to her feet.

"Well I like the stream too, especially the flowers that grow on the banks," she smiled and ironed down the front of her dress, "But I'm done now, so you can play here as long as you want."

"Oh no, you don't have to leave," Seth objected.

Annie smiled at him and shook her head, "I have to get going anyway, and I only came here for a little while to clear my head."

"Why don't you stay?" Mary pleaded and tugged on her hand.

Annie's heart warmed to the little girl, she was adorable. With big blue eyes and blonde curly hair that stuck out from under her bonnet. She was sure that Mary was Seth's ray of sunshine.

"Maybe next time, I have to go and prepare food with my sisters."

"Let go of Annie's hand Mary," Seth instructed his daughter and pried her away, "I'm sure we will meet each other again and then you can invite Mary to join you here at the stream."

"What a lovely idea," she smiled, "maybe I will pack a few eats for the next time you come here."

Little Mary nodded excitedly and Seth simply smiled at her, which caused her tummy to tumble. He was a handsome man, and probably not much older than her. Not to mention his lovely little girl.

"I will see you around some time," Annie said and then waved as she headed up the small path.

What a chance meeting, she thought. Here she was down and out and God had just revealed to her that He is still in control, and then she meets this charming little family, who despite their loss, can still smile and radiate such hope and passion that it could ignite a fire. Just to see them together warmed her heart. She looked back again and smiled as little Mary waved back at her.

Chapter 3

Seth looked at Mary where she played on the edge of the stream, floating leaves like little boats downstream. Every now and again she placed a pebble on one of the bigger leaves and when it didn't sink she squealed excitedly. She reminded him so much of Meryl, her summer blonde hair that curled like her mothers' and the dimples that indented on her cheeks when she smiled. It's been over a year since his wife had passed away from cancer, and although he accepted it a long time ago, he's only now starting to feel human again now. He had been on autopilot since her death, having had to focus on Mary and raising her, in a way he was grateful that he had his little girl. Having someone to depend on him during such a difficult time eased the hurt and pain somewhat. That was the way of life, the weak always cares for the weak, it is how God intended it. He just wishes he could have been able to save Meryl, then she could still be here watching Mary grow up.

He lay back in the grass, hitched up on one arm, He dared not question God, he knew that through the storm, God had a plan and he was going to wait on God to reveal that plan no matter how long it takes.

His thoughts shifted to the woman he had met earlier, she wasn't young enough to be unwed, and she wasn't a widow, but yet she is unattached, which he found strange. A woman with such a beautiful smile would have many possible suitors.

"Seth!" a distant voice drew him out of his reverie.

He looked up and noticed William headed his way. William was one of his friends who lived here, and whenever he came to visit, he stayed with him. He raised his hand and waved, still keeping a vigilant eye on Mary.

"Finding you is no easy task," William said as he reached him.

"You know I bring Mary here right after church whenever I'm in town," Seth said and chuckled as Mary jumped up and down to cheer on her fleet of leaves.

"She's grown up since I last saw her."

"Yes she has, but we haven't been here for some time."

"True," William nodded, "I actually came to ask if you would be up to help us out with a barn rising. Our planner, well he upped and left unexpectedly and we need someone with skill to draw up the plans."

A barn raising, it's been years since Seth had taken part in any of those, the last time he did was over three years prior to his wife's passing. He had to admit, the thought of staying here while longer was tempting. Mary will get to come here every day, he would be able to put his skills to the test, and maybe, just maybe he will be able to get to meet Annie again. That thought crept in there without warning and he quickly cleared his throat and mentally shook his head. There was no time in his life for romance; he had a daughter to care for and a business to run. As a carpenter he prided himself in the work he could do, simple yet sophisticated pieces of furniture, sold not only to the Amish community but also to outsiders who valued solid oak furniture. And with the off cuts he made small ornaments and bird houses which he sold at a local stand just outside Rothsville.

"So what happened to the other chap?" he asked curiously.

"He got tired of our ways and headed out into the world."

"That's a pity, but I guess I can hang around a little longer if you don't mind that Mary and I stay on at your place."

"Of course I won't mind, you're always welcome here you know that."

The sudden jolt of excitement made Seth grin from ear to ear. It looks like this year was a year of the Lord's favour; he will finally get to work on something significant again.

He called for Mary and she quickly came skipping towards him, she was going to be so happy to stay here, he just knew it.

"How would you like to stay here for a few weeks?" he said as he knelt down on one knee, while dusting off dry leaves and grass from her dress.

Her infectious smile spread across her face and her eyes lit up, "Really *Daed*?" she said with her child like enthusiasm, "Will I get to see Annie?"

Taken by surprise that she actually mentioned Annie, he cast a quick glance to William, who stood with his arms crossed and an amused expression on his face.

"She was here at the brook when we got here, Annie likes her," he fibbed for an excuse.

"Sure she does," William smirked.

"Can I daed, can I?" she pleaded as she hopped unto his one knee.

"I'm sure we can make a plan," he said, how could anyone say no to such a face.

As the three of them headed back up the small hill towards civilization, Seth couldn't help but think about Annie, the friendly yet mysterious woman with the radiating smile, who seemed to have captured his daughter's attention. She had never taken to any other woman like this before, not even Grace, Meryl's younger sister.

"A penny for your thoughts," William said and grinned at him.

Seth chuckled and hooked his thumbs into his suspenders, he might as well be out with it, "It's been more than a year since Meryl passed away, sooner or later Mary will need a woman to teach her how to conduct herself appropriately. Teach her how to quilt and bake bread and so on."

"And you're thinking of Annie?" Willian asked as he kicked a stone out of the way.

"Not specifically, but meeting her and seeing how much Mary enjoyed her company made me think about it."

Who was he kidding, of course he was thinking of Annie. He met some other women from his own town who were all too willing to step up and fill Meryl's shoes but he never really paid any attention to their advances. But now out of the blue, all he could seem to think of was her.

She was heaven sent, no doubt and if he didn't at least try, he would never know.

"Ay, well, Annie has had her heart broken and she's been a difficult one to get on with ever since, so good luck."

"Did it happen recently?" he asked curiously.

"About a month ago, you know the planner I told you about? Abel was his name. He just came out one day, said his good byes and left. I believe he went to New York to study science."

"And left her behind too..."

Seth felt a great deal of sympathy for her, and his heart ached. He could only imagine how much pain she must have gone through when that happened. It's one thing to send someone off to the beyond, but having someone leave out of free will to explore the world out there was like a slap in the face.

"Yeah, it was rather sad, they looked happy together."

"Clearly he was not happy, otherwise he would not have broken her heart," Seth defended.

He knew that he was going to have to take one step at a time with Annie, and not push her into anything she didn't want. But if there was one thing he would do for her, whether they ended up together or not, was to show her that God has a plan for all his children.

Chapter 4

The quietness of the early morning was peaceful, there were no birds singing their morning songs or a rooster crowing to announce the start of a new day and the sun was still buried behind the horizon. Annie closed her eyes again as the heady pull of her dreams beckoned her back to play, but she had to wake up. There was too much to do on this blessed day. The past month she spent wallowing in self-pity had robbed her of some precious time such as baking bread and taking it to the local store, not to mention her chocolate cookies everyone always used to love so much. And maybe if she was lucky, she may be able to get some of those cookies to Mary before she departed with her father.

Even for an overcast day, nothing could dispel the mood Annie was in, for the first time in weeks, she felt alive again and ready to take on the world.

"You're up early," Eva said as she entered the kitchen, "and you're baking?"

Annie smiled at her youngest sister and nodded, "Yes, it's time I stop fussing over Abel and get on with life."

Eva ran around the table and threw her arms around her neck, "Thank goodness! We were all getting so worried about you. I'm so glad you've come to your senses."

Annie laughed and hugged her sister back, it's only now that she realized just how much she inconvenienced everyone around her and she was relieved that it had all come to an end. Yes, she may still think of Abel from time to time, but it no longer affected her as it did just a day ago before God had spoken to her heart. And if she can embrace the change with a positive attitude, then she will only be blessed richly.

"I'm sorry I had you all so worried, but it's all in the past now," she said as tears sprung to her eyes.

"No need to apologize, you and Abel were together for a very long time."

Eva released her and reached for one of the cookies on the cooling rack, and then picked up her quilt basket, "I have to go, but when I get back I want to hear how on earth this paradigm shift took place."

"Of course," Annie laughed and swatted her sister's hand away, "These are for Mary, and I'll bake another batch for the house later this afternoon."

"Who's Mary? Oh wait, don't tell me, I'm going to be late, but when I get back later you can tell me everything."

And like a whirlwind Eva left the house.

Later than morning after delivering the baked flat breads to the local store Annie's mood had taken a turn for the worst, but not because of Abel. She had hoped to see Mary and Seth but it seemed that she was too later. The realization that they had left to go back to Rothsville left her empty. She should have asked them when they were leaving instead of putting in all the effort to bake cookies for Mary. A soft sigh escaped her lips as she made her way towards Anke's house, at least the cookies will be put to good use there, she thought.

"Mary!" A little voice called out to her and Anke's heart leapt with joy and she spun around.

"There you are," she smiled, "I thought you had gone back home."

"Oh no, daed said that we'll be staying here while he builds a barn," she exclaimed and hugged Annie's leg.

"She beat me to it," Seth said when he reached them.

Annie's heart fluttered in her chest and she smiled up at him, next to him the top of her head only reached his shoulder. She was just as excited as the toddler clinging to her dress having learned that they will be staying on for a while. Normally Abel would be the one drawing up the plans for the barn and making sure everything was in order. It used to be so exciting watching him loose himself I the work.

"Where will you be staying?"

"We'll be staying with William and his wife; he was kind enough to open his door for us."

"That's good yah," and she went down on her knees to get to Mary's level, "I baked you some chocolate cookies," she said holding out the small tin.

Mary beamed and immediately took the tin from Annie and dug in.

"Thank you Annie," Seth said as she stood up, "Mary has really taken to you."

"She's a lovely child."

For a moment, Annie was lost in Seth's gaze and his smile that could make the world around her fade into the background. Mary had his smile with his dimples as well as his sky blue almond shaped eyes, there was no doubt that she was his daughter. The only difference was that he had he had brown hair. His wife must have been a beautiful woman, she thought briefly before little hands drew her attention again.

"Daed said that I can stay here today while he goes to fetch our clothes, only if I stay with you."

She was so caught up in her own thoughts she never heard that part of the conversation, and the toothy grin Mary gave her arrested her.

"Well, if you don't mind leaving her with a complete stranger, then I'm happy to take care of her for you," she smiled.

"You're not a complete stranger and William did say you were good with children."

So she had been a topic of discussion between him and William? Now more than ever, she was intrigued by Seth. But if she had been the topic of discussion hen surely William had divulged the bit of information about Abel.

"Of course!" she said out loud, "You're here to take over what Abel failed to complete," she blurted out unceremoniously.

"Pardon me?"

"Abel, he used to do the plans for the barns,"

"Oh yes, Abel. That's right. William asked me to help out."

A small frown creased on his forehead and Annie almost kicked herself, that wasn't even the conversation topic. The whole thing was about her taking care of Mary.

"I'll watch Mary for you," she railed back on to the topic, "we're going to have a lot of fun."

"Will you make my hair like yours?" Mary asked and Seth laughed.

"Like mine? But what is wrong with your hair, it looks beautiful."

"It's too curly and dead can never brush it."

She looked back at Seth and he shrugged, "It's always tangled, you have no idea how difficult it is to brush her hair."

"Well I have just the solution for your problem," Annie said grinning.

The poor father had no idea how to raise a daughter, and if she could help in any way she was more than happy to.

Chapter 5

Barn raising day...

It was a fine summer's day, and the weather couldn't be more perfect. The entire community had gathered to do the barn rising for the Yoder family, who had lost their barn in a fire two months ago, and while the women were all busy making food and helping with odds and ends, the men got ready for a hard day of teamwork.

Seth stood at the table at the far side of the grounds looking over his plans again. Although raising a barn was a much bigger project that putting together tables and chairs he was confident that I was flawless.

"So word has it that you're keen on Anny," William said as he came to stand beside him.

"Is that so?" Seth chuckled.

"Yah, yah, I've heard the talk in the town. Her sister Anke actually asked me outright if I knew anything."

Seth crossed his arms over his chest and glanced towards the tables where the women were gathered. There among them all sat Annie with Mary in deep conversation. He had only been here for two weeks, and during this time he had grown fond of her. But there was always the question that poked at his conscience. Was he attracted to her simply because she got on so well with Mary, or was he attracted to her because she was, well, Annie.

"She's a pretty woman, and she's very good with children," Seth admitted, trying not to say too much.

"Come on Seth, it's more than that. She's good with children yah, but she will make a fine wife. You should go on and talk to her."

"I'm sure she does, but I don't know if she is over Abel at all."

That was a truth he could not deny. She had hardly spoken about Abel during their meets at the creek, but the way she reacted that morning when she realized that he had taken the work Abel was meant to do, indicated that he still affected her. And how would he compete with that?

"Trust me, according to Anke, her entire mood changed since the day you arrived, she just needed a shove in the right direction."

"Well at least I accomplished something," Seth joked and elbowed William, "We can jabber on about her later, right now we have a barn to finish. Are the men ready to start?"

William shook his head and chuckled, "They are all ready, but if God wills for you two to get together, you know that no power on earth or in heaven can prevent that, right?"

"Then we shall see what God has in store."

William was right about one thing, if God had his hand in this and the only reason he ended up in this community was to meet Annie, then he prayed that God's will would reign over his fleshly emotions that have been running rampant of late. If not, then he will finish this barn here today, and return to Rothsville a sane but proud father.

By the end of the day the structure stood high against the afterglow of the setting sun, and families were slowly making their way home. Seth was pleased by the work that was accomplished in one day and the fact that he was able to lay out the plans to such perfection made him proud to say the least. With only the Yoder's left along with the odd family friends, Seth made his way to where Mary was helping Annie pack away the excess food. For a moment he looked at the two of them and couldn't help but smile. Annie really did like Mary, and if he had to be honest with himself, he liked her too. She was a beautiful woman with a heart of gold and a soft spot for Mary.

Chapter 6

The barn had finally been completed, and Annie knew all too well that soon she would have to say her farewells to Seth and Mary, and that thought alone left a lump in her throat. She really liked them, especially Mary. Annie swallowed at the lump in her throat; she would never be able to have her own children, not since the unfortunately surgery when she was only twenty that left her barren. And having been able to spend these few weeks with Mary really left her wishing for a miracle.

"You should tell him how you feel," Eva said at the breakfast table.

"You mean Seth?" Annie said blushing slightly.

Eva laughed and reached for Annie's hand, "Everyone can see that you two like each other. He's a widow and you're a spinster, you're simply perfect for each other."

"I would never be so forward!" Annie exclaimed laughing, "If he feels the way everyone assume he feels, then he would have to do the ground work."

Eva raised a brow, "And if he doesn't because he is to shy?"

"Then so be it, but I am not going to embarrass myself, what if everyone is wrong about him?"

"Trust me, we're not wrong."

Eva was persistent, for one she was young and full of happily ever after dreams; secondly, she was a self-proclaimed match maker. But even if Eva was right, Annie simply refused to put herself in the firing line. It would be up to God to guide her way, not her own understanding. Her own understanding when it came to Abel didn't help one bit, so she was going to have to simply put her trust in God and hope for the best outcome.

A slight knock on the door drew the sisters' attention and Eva was the first to rush to open the door and a few seconds later, it was Seth and Mary standing in their kitchen.

"Why don't you two join us for breakfast," Eva invited.

"Oh no, we've already had breakfast," Seth said, never taking his eyes of Annie.

Eva's gaze moved from Seth to Annie and back to Seth, when she raised both brows and fought to hide a smile.

"Mary, come with me, I want to show you my room."

Relieved Annie let out breathless sigh and stood up.

"I suppose you would have to go back to your home now that the Barn is up?"

The way Seth stood shifting his weight from one foot to the other, with his head in his hand made her smile, he looked so nervous. If only he could hear the frantic beating of her own heart.

"Yah, I have to go back. I have a business to run which I have neglected while staying here," he said and looked around the kitchen.

"I'm sorry," Annie said and cleared her throat, "I'm confident that God will help you make up time for your generous act of kindness to help the Yoder's."

Without warning, Seth stepped forward and came around the table until he stood in front of her. Of course her heart stopped and the zooming bees in her stomach did not help her one bit.

"Thank you for helping out with Mary," he said with his eyes downcast.

"That was no problem at all; maybe when you come back, I can help again."

She meant it, every word. She would do anything to spend some more time with Mary and teach her how to bake and quilt. The way she felt now, she wished that this would never end. But what she wished for more was for Seth to tell her how he felt.

"I've actually been thinking," he started and Annie held her breath.

"Yes?"

"Well, you get on so well with Mary, and well, we get on well too..." he paused and shuffled closer, "I know I'm not going about this the right way, but I was thinking or rather wondering if you would like to come with us to Rothsville."

Annie's mouth fell open and she stared at him, "You mean move there?"

Seth nodded and shrugged, "We've only known each other for a short while, but when Jacob saw Rachel for the first time, he wanted to marry her right away..."

It felt as if Annie's entire world was turned on its axis and spinning in the opposite direction, did Seth just ask her to marry her or was she misunderstanding the meaning behind his words?

"What exactly are you proposing?" she said in a trembling voice.

"Oh for heaven's sake! He's asking if you'll marry him!" Eva shouted from the passageway.

Just then Mary came running out flinging her arms around Annie's legs.

Seth shrugged and smiled, "In short, yes. I mean I will go the Bishop first to ask for his blessing, but I have grown very fond of you and so has Mary, and after the time we spent together, I've come to realize that God had brought us to this place."

Her eyes shot full of tears and Eva lifted Mary up in her arms, twirling around and cheering, while her and Seth simply looked at each other.

A simple yes was all it took and Annie's dreams had come true. She found love in the strangest of circumstances and when she least expected too. On top of that, she would get to teach Mary everything that is good.

~*~

Seth could hardly have believed it was it not for the fact that he pinched himself for the umpteenth time. But there she stood, in her wedding garments. As beautiful as the first day he saw her near the brook and she was finally going to be his. But he knew that it was only by the hand of God that he had finally found a woman who will be good to both him and his daughter. And that was Annie, beautiful sweet spinster, Annie.

FOR A FIREFIGHTER'S HEART

MARISA MEYER

Chapter 1

Christine Rossouw assessed the destruction left behind by the blaze that reduced the Mulders' house to nothing but a pile of rubble and ash. It was pure luck that no one had gotten hurt in the blaze. The fire had started in the early hours of the morning when the Mulders' were still fast asleep. Now they all stood on the sidewalk, with nothing but the clothes on their back and their pet cat Malfoy, looking in horror at what was left of their home. Their belongings and their memories had literally gone up in flames. Now that was something she could never fathom, why would a family who lived day to day, turning over every penny have to endure such hardships? Why could this not happen to someone who could afford it?

It's the Lord's way to test our faith; her father's voice reminded her. To her it was more an excuse used by churchgoers to explain away logic, and logic told her a long time ago, that man's path is not destined or designed by God, but that man's path is a series of truth or dares onramps to new beginnings and disastrous endings.

She ducked under the warning tape that stretched across the front lawn, here and there, there were a few firefighters ambling around, just to ensure that the fire had been completely snuffed. Her job was to investigate the cause of the fire and fill our mounds of paperwork for insurance claims. She stepped over what used to be the threshold of the house, into what was left of it. Everything was charred black, logically, if the Mulders had all been asleep, and still managed to get down the stairs and out the front door, the fire could only have started at the back of the house or possibly the basement. Instinctively she traipsed over the rubble making her way through to the back of the house where the Laundry area used to be.

It took her close to an hour to determine the area where the blaze started and another hour to determine if it was accidental or not. In no time she had drawn the conclusion that the fire started as an electrical short in the laundry area. Apparently, Mrs. Mulder often left her tumble dryer on overnight. This, of course, would make claiming insurance a little more troublesome. Yet another flaw in the system, the insurance company is going to find every reason not to pay out the claim, by basing it on negligence, no wonder people were so up in arms with short term insurance places.

When she finally walked into her office by noon, she was finished, it's been one of those days where you barely get time to drink a cup of coffee, much less have lunch. The thought of lunch made her tummy rumble and she turned left down the hall to where the company's cafeteria was. She never ate here, but today was an exception. She had been up since 4 AM after being called out by the Fire Chief, and right now a greasy Burrito even sounded like heaven.

When she got back to her desk, there was a note that read – *Love me tender love me true, why not date me until you're blue.*

"Okay, guys! Who did it?" she asked as she crumpled up the note and dumped it in the trash.

None of them owned up but all of them laughed behind their sleeves. She knew that they all thought she was the odd one out, not being interested in dating and all. Whenever there was a company function that allowed partners, she went alone. If they all went out to drinks, she went alone. Now, it wasn't because she was anti the whole prospect of dating; it was just that she had no interest in getting tied down to one person who eventually ends up changing your character.

She had seen it so often. People lose their individuality, they change, and not for the better either, and years down the line, one or the other regret the fact that they had changed, and that's when trouble spoils paradise. Obviously, her current outlook on life came at a price. Just out of college, she dated Darryl, who was a very responsible young man with high ideals and in her opinion far-fetched dreams, but he was nice. In the beginning, like every other relationship, they both had different interests, but they both tried to get involved, she went with him to Nascar races, and he went with her to theater performances. Then they started to get comfortable and suddenly she was going to all the car races, and he came up with every excuse under the sun not to go to a theater. But it got worse, slowly but surely he started to get his back up whenever she went to the theater alone and then they ended up fighting more than anything. It was there when she finally pulled the plug on their relationship and promised herself never to date again, against her mother and fathers' wishes of course.

The ringing of her phone, drew her out of her train of thought and she reached for the receiver, "Rossouw speaking," she answered absentmindedly while she shuffled through the stack of paperwork on her desk.

"Oh, hey dad," she said and pinched the received between her shoulder and her ear. "Mmm no, I haven't forgotten... yeah... mmm... well, I'm kind of busy... I know, I said I would be there but something came up... seriously, dad, it's not like the church is going to run away... Okay fine, I'll be there... yeah, I love you too."

She pulled out the incident report from one of the arson cases she had to submit to the lawyer and shoved it into the out basket, then dropped her head on her arms. She loved her parents, but her dad was forever begging her to go to church. Another place she tries to avoid at all cost. Church people were probably the most hypocritical beings alive, she thought despondently, but she knew that if she went to this one service, they would leave her alone for several months before they begged her to visit again. So she was going to simply suck it up, go, and get it over and done with.

Chapter 2

Jarod looked at himself in the mirror as he fixed his tie, it was still a while before the church would start, but he preferred to be the first one in and the first one out, usually picking the last pew right in the corner. He had a very trying time after his divorce, nearly lost his job and everything he had, because of it. Was it not for Pastor Rossouw who helped him to see the light, he would still be staring at the bottom of the bottle. He was never much of a drinker during his marriage, but after he found out that Elaine cheated on him, he drowned his sorrows, the only way he knew how. It's been two years since they went their separate ways and it was just like Pastor Rossouw had said, his hatred had turned to indifference, and the love he once felt for Elaine had subsided. He often saw her in town, but there was no more anger or bitterness. The point is that they were two different people, and in the end, they simply drifted apart. Elaine wanted kids and a house with a white picket fence, two dogs, and an SUV, with a husband that worked nine to five. He couldn't give her that, not at the time anyway. So, as a result, she went out and found what she wanted. He was happy for her, he truly was, but he promised himself that he would never marry again and committed himself to the fact that he would focus on work and God.

"Morning Jarod," Pastor Rossouw greeted as he unlocked the church.

"Morning Pastor, lovely day today, isn't it?"

"Indeed, we need the rain; hopefully it's here to stay for a few days."

The unexpected gift of rain had been a blessing after weeks of drought and unbearable heat, and although the rainy season was still a few weeks ago, the skies didn't lie. Jarod loved the rain.

"According to the weather, we can expect rainfall for at least three days," he chuckled and then entered the church and waited for the pastor to turn the lights on.

"Are you going to move up a pew?" Pastor Rossouw asked.

Jarod shook his head and smiled, "Maybe next time."

The pastor didn't push him, but he always asked him out of interest more than anything, that was the extent of their conversations. More small talk really. The pastor went on about his business and Jarod took a seat in his usual spot, waiting patiently for the pews to fill up.

Today, however, with the rain falling, he didn't expect the church to be packed. He always found it rather odd how people would run about in the rain to get to Walmart or go places, but the moment it rains they use it as an excuse to skip church.

One by one individual and families arrived, filling the pews from the front of the church towards the back. Two youngsters came bolting down the side aisle and darted between a couple talking in the front, then they disappeared under the pews. No one seemed to be perturbed by their playfulness, which he liked. Then again the sign right above the small stage read – Let the little children come to me, and do not hinder them.

He turned his attention back to the small hymnal in his hands, and paged aimlessly through it, trying to appear preoccupied, in the hope that no-one tried to make any conversation with him. But his hopes were dashed with Pastor Rossouw spoke next to him.

"Jarod, I would like you to meet Christine, my daughter."

Jarod stood up and wiped his hand on the back of his jeans and then extended it to the woman in front of him. She was beautiful, tall with long blond hair that flowed loosely over her shoulders. But the smile that tugged at the corner of her lips didn't reach her light blue eyes. It was as if the lights were on but nobody was home, she was just going through the motions.

"It's a pleasure to meet you, Christine," he said and shook her hand firmly.

"It's a pleasure," she repeated his words and removed her hand.

"Jarod is a firefighter, I thought you two would have a lot in common," Pastor Rossouw piped up and Jarod wanted to shrink away, but he remained poised.

"You're also in the department?" he asked out of interest.

"Not exactly, I'm in forensics, I investigate the aftermath and the cause of the fire," she answered.

"Nice," he said, not sure what else to add.

He felt awkward with her, not in a negative kind of way, but purely because he hasn't spoken to a woman on a casual basis since before he was married. And when the pastor walked away leaving the two of them alone in each other's company, he shrugged and stepped back.

"You can sit here if you want?" he offered.

This time she smiled, "I won't mind at all, anything but sitting right in the front where my dad wants me."

Jarod chuckled and moved over two spaces, leaving enough space between them. They sat in silence for a while before Christine spoke.

"You have to excuse my dad, he can be very forward at times," she smiled, "He keeps wanting to set me up for dates."

Jarod laughed at that, "Playing pastor and matchmaker, I see."

She rolled her eyes, "Yeah, he does it every time I set foot in a church, which is why I'm never here," she turned to look at him, "I haven't seen you here before, though."

He shrugged, "I've been here a few months now, but I don't stay around to mingle with the members. I just come for my daily bread and then I disappear."

"Ah, I see," she said, "The dash and go type."

"Yeah, that would be me."

"You do know that church is meant for communion and encouragement from fellow Christians."

He leaned forward with his elbows on his knees and regarded the congregation, "I come here to learn and find peace."

"A man with depth, well I'm sure you'll find peace being stuck here in the back all the time."

"It's worked so far."

Throughout the service, Jarod was acutely aware of the woman who was seated next to him. The aroma of her perfume kept wafting past him, making him shift uncomfortably in his seat. By the time the service came to an end, he couldn't wait to get out. He needed fresh air and fast.

"Well Jarod, it was a nice having company here at the back," Christine said as she stood up to let him pass.

"Yeah, it was," he dragged his hand over his stubbly short hair, "I'll see you around?"

All she did was nod, and that was his queue. He exited this church like a bolt of lightning.

Chapter 3

Christine did not expect that at all. She knew her father was up to something when he insisted on her coming to church. She was prepared for the worst, him introducing her to another pastor, or one of the deacons, or worst case, preaching hellfire and brimstone to try and get her to get back into the habit of going to church. The last thing she expected was to be introduced to a firefighter. And not just any firefighter, Jarod Marks had all the bits and pieces that would make any woman turn into a fan-girl. He was built like an MMA fighter, he had deep willow green eyes and brown, almost black hair that was neatly trimmed and on top of that, he had that five o'clock shadow that danced across his chin, making him look even manlier than he possibly could. For the first time in years, she wondered if her anti-dating motto was even viable. Just because she made one bad choice in life, by dating Darryl, didn't mean that every man she met would be like him.

After the service, she had spoken to her dad and tried to find out more about Jarod, of course, her dad was all too happy to tell her that he's a firefighter, with a deep soul, but beyond that, he didn't want to divulge any personal information. He did, however, mention that Jarod had also been in a bad relationship that left him weary of dating, much like her.

So what if he was damaged goods, she, though, he couldn't possibly be more damaged than she was.

Thankfully thinking about Jarod and the possibility of entering the dating scene again was a momentarily lapse in judgment, but the next day, she had once again gotten her mind focused on work and making sure she didn't fall into the dating trap again. Or so she thought. Every now and again, when she wasn't going through case files or looking at labs of fire starters that contained possible chemicals, Jarod's face floated into her mind. It got to a point where she went for her second visit to the cafeteria in one week, which was totally out of character. This time she opted for a slice of cheesecake and strong coffee.

"Rossouw!" one of her colleagues called. "Having a love affair with that cheesecake?"

"Shut it, Kemp," she mumbled and took a generous scoop out of spite and shoved it all into her mouth.

Dalton Kemp came over and pulled the chair out, plonking himself down, "You really need to get out more, we're having a get-together tonight at Franks' are you coming around?"

Franks was a bar not too far from the office, where they staff often went to wind down after a rough day at the office. Most of the time she opted out of going to mingle, but tonight was an exception, she needed a distraction.

"Yeah sure, I'll see you there at around seven."

"Great, bring your date," Kemp chuckled and dug her coffee spoon into her cheesecake.

"Hey! Stop that," she muttered and pulled her plate away.

One thing about her line of work and the people she worked with was that they were all like family. And this was the only family where she felt she belonged. Back at home, with her mom and dad, she felt like the odd one out, simply because she didn't share in their beliefs. She used to, but it all changed in her first year of being a firefighter. It was during that year, where she realized that God helps who he wants to. She had seen too many tragic deaths that included young children and elderly people to think that there was anything merciful about God. After a year of being a firefighter, she eventually opted to take a job in forensics and fire investigations and was transferred. Now instead of running into burning buildings to save people, she now investigated the aftermath instead.

At around noon, after her last case file was concluded, she locked her office and made her way to Franks' to join the others. The atmosphere was festive and the place was crowded. She spotted her colleagues at the far end near the back of the pup and wrangled her way through the crowd.

"Rossouw! You made it, where's Mr. Cheesecake?" Kemp called out raising his beer to her.

She rolled her eyes and laughed, "We had a fight, I left him in the cafeteria to bond with Miss Caramel," she joked.

She ordered herself a cola since she wasn't really one for drinking and joined the rest. The mood was light, and no one spoke about work, which was a relief. She opted for a seat at the far end of the table next to Janet, the receptionist, who was a gray little mouse who barely spoke as it was. She was a bit of an introvert, so other than sipping on her drink she didn't add much value to the conversation. But Christine didn't mind that at all.

It was a while later when a sudden explosion ripped through the kitchen and an orange flame punched its way into the main bar area. Windows shattered and people fell to the ground as smoke and fire billowed into the establishment. Caroline grabbed Jannet and pulled her down to the ground almost instantly as panic erupted. Everywhere people were trying to make it out of the bar, some managing just before the flames engulfed the front entrance.

"Bathroom!" Christine cried out as she tugged Janet's arm, practically dragging her along the side of the wall towards the back where the restrooms were. With any luck they could find a way out through one of the small windows, worst cases they would have water.

The fire alarms erupted over and above the agonizing cries of everyone stuck in the building and Christine knew that if they made it out of here alive, it would be a miracle. Her hope to find an escape route through one of the smaller windows was futile, she might fit through one at a squeeze but Janet won't and she refused to leave the young girl behind. Huddled in the corner of the bathroom, with her arms wrapped around the frantic girl, she could only hope that someone will get to them in time. For the first time in years, she prayed for help.

Christine thought fast, she pulled off her top and drenched it with water, then handed it to Janet, "Here, keep this over your mouth and nose, try to take shallow breaths okay?"

She then grabbed her denim jacket and did the same. Smoke was starting to fill the bathroom and the heat from the main room was slowly pushing towards the back. Time was of the essence, and if the fire department did not arrive soon, they would all meet their maker.

"We're going to die!" Janet panicked.

"No we're not, help is on its way," Christine shouted over the noise of crackling flames and falling banisters.

The sound of approaching sirens was a relief to some extent, at least the fire department was here, but the question that plagued her, was if they would get to them in time. Christine assessed their situation. The fire hadn't reached the restrooms yet, but the heat was excruciating, and smoke pummeled into the small room stealing all the oxygen. She instructed Janet to stay put while she crawled out from under the sink, keeping her body bowed low on the ground. She needed to get to one of the windows and call for help. She felt her way around the floor until she reached one of the cubicles, and then she clambered her way to the window.

"Help! We're in here!" she shouted between bouts of coughs and heaving for air. Her throat was burning and her lungs were filled with smoke, but she refused to give up, "Help!" she called again and again.

"Over here!" she heard someone shout and only then did she allow herself to collapse on the floor. At least now someone would try to get to them.

The last thing she remembered was the incessant smoke that filled the room and the unbearable heat that licked at her skin before her entire world went black.

"Christine! Stay with me!" she recognized the voice from somewhere but she couldn't quite place it, "Christine can you hear me?"

She tried to respond but she simply couldn't. Her brain was doing all the work but the signal to the rest of her body was down. She kept drifting in and out of consciousness but the cool air that surrounded her meant that she was no longer in the inferno. That, or she had died and gone to, wherever bad girls go.

"Where is the ambulance!" she heard her savior call out.

"J... Janet," she managed to utter.

"She's responsive! Christine, it's Jarod, you've had some smoke inhalation, do you know where you are?" she heard him asked.

She tried to open her eyes, but it felt like a million cinders were stuck to her eyeballs, "Where is Janet," she asked first and foremost.

"She's fine, she's alive, thanks to you," he said and squeezed her hand, "But now we need to take care of you."

"Jarod?" she asked half deliriously, "From church?"

He chuckled and brushed her hair from her face, "Yeah Jarod from church, now save your breath. The ambulance will take you to the hospital; I'll come by later to check up on you."

She reached blindly for his hand and squeezed it, "Thank you," she whispered as her head spun and she once again plummeted into a dark hole.

Chapter 4

Jarod was the first to arrive at the hospital, followed by Christine's mom and dad, who both looked like they had been crying.

"Pastor Rossouw..." Jarod started.

"Call me James," he said to Jarod and then introduced his wife, "This is Marjorie, have you heard anything?"

He shook his head, "No I haven't, I'm not family but I know that she had inhaled a lot of smoke, but thankfully the fire never reached them."

"Oh thank you, Lord," her mother exclaimed casting her eyes to the heavens.

"Christine was very brave," Jarod said as he told the couple how she burrowed into the restrooms with her colleague, using very basic methods to keep from suffocating, "When she decided to call for help, was when she inhaled most of the smoke. But if she hadn't done that, no one would have known they were in the bathroom."

Marjorie sat down and cupped her hand over her mouth and James sat down beside her, wrapping his arm around her shoulders, "You were heaven sent," he said to Jarod, "Thank you for saving our little girl."

Jarod smiled and shook his head, "I was just doing my duty sir Pastor."

He left the couple and made his way down the corridor to get some coffee, he was still in uniform, covered in soot and smelling like a furnace, but he didn't want to go until he was a hundred percent sure that Christine was out of danger.

A while later he returned and made his way to where Christine's room was, through the window he saw the Pastor and his wife talking to Christine, who looked like hell but beautiful all the same. She was alive, and by the looks of it, recovering. Thankfully she didn't sustain any burns, it could have been so much worse.

Christine had spotted him just as he was about to leave and waved him over. When he entered the room, her mom and dad excused themselves to go get a bite to eat.

"How are you feeling?" he asked as he pulled a chair closer.

"Like a pizza base right out of the oven?" she said and laughed, but then coughed and clutched her chest, "change that, I feel like I've been to hell and back."

Jarod chuckled and handed her a glass of water, "It was quite something you did back there, your dad mentioned to me you were a firefighter before."

She took a sip of water and counted her breaths, "Yeah, for a year, then I moved to fire forensics."

"I'm glad you didn't forget the training then, it came in handy," he commented.

Even as she lay there, pale as a sheet, with her blond hair still covered in soot and ash, she was beautiful. He never thought that he would even look at another woman after his wife cheated on him, and here he was, doing just that.

He cleared his throat and made an effort to leave, but Christine caught his arm, and smiled, "I owe you dinner and a movie," she said half smiling.

He chuckled and nodded, "As soon as you're back on your feet, I'll come to collect."

Soon he was ushered away when the nurses entered to do the general BP checks, but for a moment he stood looking at her over their heads.

"And the Lord God said, It is not good that a man should be alone," a disembodied voice sounded and Jarod turned to respond, but there was no one else around, other than the nurses going about their business.

Puzzled he turned and looked back at Christine and then waved and left. This was the strangest thing he had ever experienced. It was as if there was someone else there with him, someone far more enlightened than he was. But the words stuck to him all the way home. And he realized beyond a shadow of a doubt that Christine did not appear in his life out of mere coincidence. This was something far bigger than him, or anyone else for that matter.

Chapter 5

Within a few days, Christine was discharged from hospital and sent home to recover. On her mother's insistence, she had no choice but to spend another week staying her folks until she was strong enough to return to work, but every day, Jarod made an effort to visit her, and if he couldn't get to her physically, he would call her. At first, she thought nothing of it, assuming that he was simply being nice, but out of the blue, every time her phone rang and his caller ID flickered on her screen, her stomach would rumble with excitement. Or when she heard his car pull up, she could hardly contain herself. Her dad, of course, wasn't blind either. He knew exactly what was going on.

"Jarod's a fine young man," he said one morning over coffee.

"Yeah, he's nice," she mumbled into her cup.

"Do you like him?"

She whipped her head around and looked at her dad, but the way he smiled at her disarmed her completely and she felt a blush creep into her cheeks, "Yeah, a little."

Her dad chuckled, and Christine put her cup down, "How do you know when you meet the right person?" she asked.

Her dad took his reading glasses off and regarded her, "That's a tough one on answer sweetheart, but sometimes you just know."

She worried her lip and looked into the distance. She had spent all this time guarding her own heart against heartbreak and disappointment. For so long she refused to believe that love existed and convinced herself that she didn't need anyone to go home too. But tragedy has a way to open one's eyes and this is exactly what happened to her. While she was trapped in that restroom practically staring death in the face, her first instinct was to pray and ask God to help her and Janet out of that pickle. It was at that point where she remembered to use what she had to her advantage. And not once during that entire time while they were stuck in that room did she panic, it was an ethereal calm that had taken over and now that she has had time to think it over, she could only come to one conclusion. God had sent His angels to help them. And she was convinced that Jarod was one of them, her personal angel. The thought of him warmed up her heart and a smile spread across her face.

"Penny for your thoughts?" her dad asked.

"I think it's time I go back to church," she said, "and I think I want to give love a chance."

Her dad put his book down and turned to her, smiling, "It's only when you leap into the water that you learn to swim sweetheart. Trust in the Lord and he will make a way clear for you."

Her dad always had wise comebacks, and although she still had a lot to overcome, she knew that little baby steps would eventually get her there.

At around noon, Jared's car rumbled outside, and Christine gave herself one last once-over in the mirror. It was date night, and she was nervous. She tucked a stray strand of hair back into place pulled her lips into a tight pout and released it. It felt as if the muscles in her face were refusing to cooperate.

"Honey!" her mom called and she took a deep steadying breath before making her way to the living room.

When she saw Jared, her heart did that familiar tumble, "Hi," she said and mentally rolled her eyes at her own silliness, "I mean, welcome?" she shook her head, "Never mind, are you ready to go?"

Jared chuckled and nodded at her dad and her mom, "We won't be out very late," he said and Christine literally dragged him out of the house.

"Are you okay?" he asked with a hint of humor in his voice.

"Do I look okay?" she chirped.

"You look fine to me."

Her internal thermometer was about to pop. The way he looked at her when he said she looked fine made her feel all warm and fuzzy inside. She reminded herself that she wasn't a teenager on a first date and forced to compose herself.

"I'm sorry, I just, I haven't been on a date in ages," she said as he opened the passenger door for her.

"Well that makes two of us, so trust me, there's no need to be nervous."

That was a relief she thought, but still, her heart kept thrumming against her chest.

Jarod had surprised her with a visit to a local musical arts theater, where they were hosting a fundraiser for a little girl who needed a skin graph after having sustained serious burns when she was caught in a burning car. Again, he had completely swept her feet out from under her, and she was in complete awe by how passionate he was.

"So do you always get involved in these fundraisers?" she asked curiously over dessert.

He chuckled and reached to wipe a smudge of cream from her chin, "Not always, it depends on the nature of the campaign. Sarah has a special place in my heart, she was only four when the car they were traveling in was involved in a head-on collision. Besides the fact that she was trapped in the burning car, she lost both her parents."

Christine swallowed at the lump in her throat, "That's terrible; I can't even begin to imagine how hard that must be for her."

This was exactly what she couldn't understand, why God would allow such a thing to happen, was just too cruel to comprehend.

"There's actually more to the story than most would believe," he said quietly, "You see, her parents were both alcoholics, and there were a few cases of child abuse against them, but the system failed her. But the funny thing is, after the accident, the driver of the other car, who survived, decided to adopt her and they are paying for all her medical bills."

Christine's jaw dropped and she blinked at the tears that threatened to spill.

"That's nothing short of a miracle," she said softly.

"You can say that again. It's true, God works in mysterious ways, and we don't always know the answers, but He does."

She was both shocked and thrilled by the news, and she couldn't help but cry. Jarod shifted his chair closer to hers and wrapped his arm around her shoulder.

"I didn't mean to make you cry, this is supposed to be the first date," he whispered.

"You didn't make me cry, it's just that," she sniffed against his shoulder, "all this time I figured God was merciless, never once did I consider a bigger picture."

"Shhh," Jarod comforted her and held her close, "It sometimes takes an extraordinary event to make us see things through His eyes, and all I know is that God never fails us, it's only our own expectations."

Chapter 6

Christine took a deep steadying breath as she stood at the end of the aisle, her dad by her side, and Jarod waiting in front, wearing his step out fireman's uniform with all his decorated medals. To the left were all his mates, and the entire squadron of firefighters some wearing their uniforms, other also wearing step outs, to the right was her family and some of her colleagues.

Her big day had arrived; she was finally going to promise herself to the one man she was willing to trust with her life. The wedding march started and she counted her steps in her mind, like a waltz down the aisle.

"I'm so proud to be your father," her dad whispered without moving his lips.

"Daddy you make me proud," she said, "thank you for introducing me to Jared."

Her insides were a kaleidoscope of butterflies and as her father handed her over to her future husband, she couldn't her fingers from trembling, but Jared took her hands in his and smiled at her. His eyes mirrored the same love she felt, and instantly he calmed her down.

It was a day to remember, Christine had not only promised herself to the love of her life, she also found God somewhere in the mix. Somewhere along the line, she realized that God never left; all she had to do was turn around and call on Him.

Christine and Jared lived happily ever after, doing what they both loved and in each other, they found the missing puzzle pieces that made them both complete.

"Are we going to go for green or yellow?" Christine asked holding up two cans of paint.

"Why not do both," Jared said as he worked at assembling the crib.

"Mmm, good point," she said and placed the two small tins on the coffee table, "how is the crib coming along?"

Jared stood up discarding the spanner and pulled his pregnant wife into his arms, "I think we just get our baby to share our bed for a while," he chuckled.

Christine laughed and wrapped her arms around her husband's neck, "I love you," she murmured against his lips.

"And I love you, Christine Marks," Jared said and kissed her.

HAVE FAITH IN ME

MALLORY LOVE

Chapter One – Love Prevails

Jill Goodman laced her long, elegant fingers together in her lap. Before her was a familiar sight. Students were seated at their desks, whispering amongst themselves, although their teacher had instructed them to be quiet. Despite her many efforts, the children never showed any respect for authority. She was drowning and she could not come up for air.

Working at St. Margaret's Reformatory House had taught her a lot about troubled youth, but it had not taught her how to cure them. No matter how much she listened and disciplined them, they still acted out in some of the most unimaginable ways. It pained her to see so little progress, but there was not much that she could do. She followed the handbook. She taught them the Scripture. The troubled teenagers had left her hopeless.

One student, in particular, was acting up so frequently that the school asked Jill to sit in on his classes to observe his behavior. Even though this made it difficult to balance her many appointments, she agreed to it. Every student mattered, and she would do whatever it took to help them find inner peace.

A loud snicker came from the corner where her student was seated. He was alone and appeared to be working on his assignment, yet the mischievous grin on his face said that he was up to no good. Jill narrowed her eyes. Then, he let out another cackle.

"Is something funny, Mr. Schwartz?" Mrs. Romero asked, raising a drawn-on eyebrow. "Would you like to share it with the class?"

The student's face flushed and he hurriedly tried to tuck away the paper. Mrs. Romero got to her feet and started shuffling down the aisle.

"Ooooh!" the class howled as she closed in on him.

"I'll take that," she hissed, grabbing the paper from his hands. "Now let's see what's so funny."

Then, all of a sudden, her face fell.

"Well, if that's what you think about this class, how about you spend the rest of the afternoon in the headmaster's office?"

"Whatever," he grunted, seizing his belongings. "I'd rather be there than here."

"Excuse me, young man?" Mrs. Romero spat. Her eyes then flashed to the counselor. "Ms. Goodman, are you seeing this?"

Jill nodded, a sad smile on her face. She scribbled down some notes, though there was nothing that she could write down that would change Brandon. After working with the troubled student for over a year with little to no progress, she had come to the conclusion that Brandon needed divine intervention.

Brandon shuffled out of the classroom. Mrs. Romero followed him into the hall, her hand on hip, just to make sure he actually headed in the right direction. It was not unlike Brandon to ditch a trip to the headmaster's office altogether by spending several hours in the bathroom. He had been caught ditching classes there several times in the past, despite Jill's constant reminders that avoiding problems would not solve them.

It was students like Brandon that made Jill question her career choice.

Lonesome dinners were becoming part of Jill's everyday routine. While she used to meet with coworkers, nobody was interested anymore. Many of them were now married and she detested being the third wheel. She never knew how difficult it would be to be single in her late thirties.

Once upon a time, her career had been enough to keep her occupied. She had been a hopeful young woman with high expectations for herself and the teenagers she desperately wanted to help. With so much on her plate, men were the last thing on her mind. She needed to be focused for the kids, and surely a man would just be a distraction.

Seven years later, all of her time and energy had not yet paid off. Though melancholy plagued her every time she looked at the empty seat across the table, she had to remember it was all for a good cause. She was helping young people. It was the duty that God bestowed upon her and whether she felt appreciated or not, she was to fulfill it.

"Here's to another night alone, Bo-Bo," she murmured to her Golden Retriever, who was sprawled out underneath the table. "At least I have you."

She scrubbed him behind the ears.

"I wish my kids appreciated me the way you do," she admitted with a sigh. "You're always happy to see me."

Bo-Bo looked up at her with admiration in his eyes. A tear ran down her cheek.

"Good boy, buddy. Good boy."

The next morning, Jill drove to work as usual. Her rickety sedan groaned in protest during the fifteen-minute drive and even stalled at the single stoplight between her house and St. Margaret's. She could only hope that her day would get better. Unfortunately, it didn't.

As soon as she got to her office, she found a barely legible note on her door.

Emergency meeting @ 8AM. Brandon Schwartz and Parents.

Jill disliked meeting with parents ever since she started her career at St. Margaret's. Parents oftentimes blamed her for their children's continual disobedience; they questioned her professionalism. Parent meetings were one of the most discouraging parts of her job. It was not the morning that she wanted to be dealing with one.

She fiddled with her keys until she found the right one and unlocked her office. As she stepped inside, her bright blue eyes flickered towards the clock on the wall. It was already half past seven. She felt her heart leap into her chest.

Brandon is a problem child. They'll understand, she thought to herself. *I just have to explain his behavior in the classroom. They'll realize it's not my fault.*

She sat down at her desk and put her face in her hands.

Even though it probably is my fault, she second guessed herself. *It's my job to fix him—to make him better. I can't even do my job right!*

The minute hand moved. Eight o' clock was imminent.

There was a knock on the door. Jill glanced at the clock on the wall and took a deep breath. It was three minutes 'til eight.

"You're early!" she announced, opening the door with a wide, false smile. "Come in, come in!"

Mr. and Mrs. Schwartz accepted her invitation and followed her into her small office. They each sat across from her in the small plastic chairs meant for students. Brandon stood behind them, hiding his face behind his mother's tall, red up-do.

"We were a bit confused when Headmaster Fitzgerald called us," Mrs. Schwartz admitted, pursing her red lips. "Brandon has been so well-behaved at home. Frankly, I was surprised he was getting into any trouble at school at all."

Jill's stomach churned.

"Well, we aren't sure what it is that is triggering Brandon either, Mrs. Schwartz. That's what we would like to find out," she explained. "Now, I've had many meetings with Brandon and he does not seem to know what is causing him to act like this either."

Mr. Schwartz furrowed his brow and asked, "Isn't that your job?"

Jill's face flushed.

"W-well, you see, Brandon seems to find it funny when—"

"So is that what this is all about? Pointing fingers at my son?" Mrs. Schwartz spat, crossing her arms.

"No, ma'am! Of course not! We just—"

"I don't pay fifteen thousand dollars a year for you to ruin all of the progress we've made at home," Mr. Schwartz asserted. "If he is acting fine at home, why is he a problem in school? He should be focused. Now, if the school is less equipped to handle my boy than we are, maybe we should just pull him out and homeschool him!"

Brandon raised his eyebrows.

"Please?" he begged. "I'd rather be at home than here."

"Shut up, you!" Mrs. Schwartz hissed. "I wasn't talking to you."

Brandon's face fell.

"Well, what we can suggest is an extra Scripture class," Jill murmured, leaning forward. "Now, if Brandon was willing to spend some extra time after class—"

"What? No way!" Brandon exclaimed, incredulously.

Mrs. Schwartz raised a bushy, red eyebrow.

"Scripture, you say? And you think this would help?"

Jill peered into Brandon's file and nodded.

"I think it could do Brandon a lot of good," she said. She smiled and added, "After all, love prevails over evil."

Mrs. Schwartz furrowed her brow and asked, "Are you calling my son evil?"

Jill's face became a deep shade of scarlet as she shook her head.

"No, no, of course not! I just was saying—"

"Well," Mrs. Schwartz interrupted, glaring at her son, "if you think it'd help, we're willing to give it a try. Maybe he can take an extra Sunday school class too."

Brandon rolled his eyes.

"Mom!"

"'Mom' nothing!" she scolded. "You're going to after-school Scripture class and that's that. If this school can do one thing right, it's making sure you learn your Bible."

The dark-haired boy groaned.

"Fine...but I don't have to like it!"

Chapter Two – Back in Town

There was one place that Jill could find solace no matter how underappreciated and lonely that she felt: church.

Dressed in her Sunday best, Jill opened the grand, mahogany double doors and sauntered inside the grand house of worship. The navy carpet welcomed her in, as always. The church always wrapped her in a warm hug. She could feel God over her shoulder. It was right where she needed him.

Several other members of the church embraced her and asked her about work, a subject that she very much wished to avoid. After politely ignoring their questions, she quietly seated herself far away from her mom's usual spot. While she was ready for Pastor John's opening prayer, she was not ready to face her coworkers, the Schwartz family, or even her mother. She hoped to hide in plain sight.

Churchgoers quickly filled the pews and Jill sunk into her seat. The past week had been difficult and she just wanted to pray in peace. The faster that Paster John's sermon started the better.

As Paster John neared his podium, she could finally relax. He stopped to speak with a volunteer. She groaned.

Then, she felt a tap on her shoulder.

Gritting her teeth, she turned around to see who it was trying to get her attention. To her surprise, it was Meredith Blau. Despite their many years of going to the same church, she had not spoken to Meredith since they were teenagers.

"Yes?" Jill asked, her expression softening.

"Have you seen who's here?" Meredith hissed.

Jill frowned and replied, "No? Who?"

"Adam Panton," Meredith whispered. "Didn't you two used to date in high school?"

Jill's heart sank. She had dated Adam in high school, but they were not on good terms when they broke up after their senior year. In fact, Jill had hardly dated since they ended their relationship. Adam had made it difficult for her to trust men, and that was when she decided to put her career first.

"Yes we did," Jill muttered. "Years ago."

Before she and Meredith could further discuss the complexities of her high school relationship, Pastor John stepped up to the podium and started his Sunday morning announcements. To Jill's dismay, nobody was going to let her forget about Adam anytime soon.

"As our regular members know, the spaghetti dinner for Molly Newhart's family will be this Thursday. Please bring donations if you can. Let's have a moment of silence for the Newhart family now."

The room was silent for a moment.

"Amen," Pastor John murmured.

"Amen," the crowd followed suit.

Pastor John cleared his throat and continued, "Also, I would like everyone to please welcome a hometown hero! Adam Panton! Please stand up so everyone can say hello to the town's best quarterback to ever set foot on the field!"

Everyone clapped—except Jill. Her eyes bore into the back of his head as he waved to the crowd as though he had just won a major beauty pageant. She could not believe he would have the audacity to show his face in her church.

The crowd died down and Pastor John continued.

"Sadly, Mr. Panton has recently been diagnosed with an illness we can only hope will be healed by God. I would appreciate if you would all join me in a silent prayer for Mr. Panton and his family."

Jill gasped, earning several disapproving looks from other church members.

Is he sick? she thought to herself. No, he can't be...

Pastor John interrupted her thoughts.

"Amen."

"Amen."

It was church tradition for prominent members to stay after and eat dinner together. While less-involved members sometimes joined, it was not common. Jill was almost positive that Adam wouldn't dare show his face at an after-service dinner. To her misfortune, she was wrong.

She was scooping a large pile of potatoes onto her plate as Pastor John wrapped a comforting arm around her shoulders. She smiled at him.

"Your sermon was beautiful today, Pastor John," she said. "As always."

"Oh thank you, Jill," he replied. He then raised his bushy, gray brows and asked, "Have you met Adam? I spoke about him in the sermon—Adam! Adam! Over here! I have someone I want you to meet!"

Before Jill could protest, the tall, square-jawed blond sauntered towards her.

"Adam, this is J—"

"Jill Goodman," Adam interrupted a smirk on his face. "It's been a long time."

Jill forced a smile and murmured, "Yeah. A long time."

"So you two know each other then?" Pastor John asked. "I guess I'll let you catch up, then. God bless."

He pushed past them both, a full plate in his hand. Jill looked down at her feet. Without Pastor John around to cut the tension, she had no way to control her anger.

"You decided to come back."

Adam laughed.

"Nice to see you too!" he jested. His voice softened. "Look, I know things didn't exactly work out with us, but if you would just hear me out—"

"What?" Jill snapped. "Because you're rich? Because you're sick? You don't get to just come to my church and tell me what I have to listen to. You sure didn't care what I had to say fifteen years ago. Why should I care what you have to say now?"

He sighed.

"Y-yeah, you're right. I'm sorry. I didn't know what I was thinking coming here. I'll uh—I'll just get going. Take care, Jill."

With that, he brushed by her and made his way out of the small cafeteria. Pastor John came back to Jill's side, a frown on his face.

"Where'd Adam go?" he asked.

Jill gave him a sad smile.

"He uh—he had someplace to be," she replied.

Pastor John pursed his lips and nodded.

"He's a busy man—what with the chemo treatments and all."

Jill gulped.

"Chemo?" she asked.

Pastor John raised his brows.

"Well, yes. Prayer warriors help, but he needs chemotherapy too. He's facing a battle greater than himself right now. He needs all the help he can get."

"So it's cancer, then," Jill confirmed, dejectedly. "When you said he was ill—that's what you meant. He has cancer."

Pastor John nodded.

"I'm afraid so."

Jill's telephone had been ringing off the hook. The only person that ever called her was her mother, but she did not even want to talk to her. She even disconnected her answering machine. Ever since she heard that Adam had cancer, she was trying to determine how she felt about it. Their history told her that she should loathe him, yet she couldn't.

Bo-Bo howled at the ringing telephone and Jill scowled.

"Okay, fine! Fine!" she shouted. "I'm picking it up!"

She picked up the phone and pressed the answer button.

"Hello?"

"Jill!"

"Hi Mom," Jill grumbled.

"You haven't been answering your phone," Mrs. Goodman noted. "Is something wrong?"

"No, nothing's wrong," Jill murmured. "Just been working a lot."

"And avoiding my calls," Mrs. Goodman retorted. "I didn't see you in church the other day. Did you stay home this past Sunday?"

"No," Jill grumbled. "I was just sitting somewhere else."

"Aha! Avoiding me! Just like I said!" Mrs. Goodman accused. "Ah well, I can't say I'm surprised. Anyway, how are you? How is work?"

"It's work," Jill said.

"And how are you feeling about Adam being in town?"

There it is! Jill thought to herself. I knew she wanted something!

"I'm done fine," Jill replied through gritted teeth. "Is that what you've been calling me about?"

There was a short silence on the other end of the phone.

"Mom?"

"Yes, dear. I'm here. And no, of course, that's not the only reason I've been trying to call you. I just—I just thought you might want to talk about it."

"Talk about what?" Jill snapped. "He broke my heart fifteen years ago and then he waltzed into my church like nothing happened. He's an idiot and I'd rather not discuss him, so if we could please talk about something else, that'd be great."

Mrs. Goodman sucked on her teeth.

"Well, if you're going to have an attitude, I suppose I'll just talk to you another time," she murmured. "Love you."

"Love you too," Jill groaned.

She hung up the phone and buried her face in her hands.

Chapter Three – Apology

On Wednesday, Brandon was absent from Mrs. Romero's class. Confused, Jill ran to the headmaster's office. There had to be an explanation.

"E-excuse me," she stammered, partially out of breath. "Katie?"

The secretary looked up from her computer screen.

"Yes? What is it, Ms. Goodman?" she asked.

"Brandon Schwartz. He should've been in Mrs. Romero's classroom, but he was absent. I was wondering if his parents called in?" Jill asked, wringing her hands.

Katie's fingers rushed across the keyboard. She shook her head.

"Mrs. Romero should've gotten an email. The Schwartzes pulled Brandon out of St. Margaret's yesterday."

Jill furrowed her brow.

"Is he sick?"

Katie shook her head.

"When I say they pulled him out, I meant for good. Brandon won't be coming back. Like I said, Mrs. Romero should've gotten an email."

Jill's face fell.

"They...they withdrew him?"

Katie nodded.

"I uh—I need to go," Jill replied, hurriedly.

She turned on her heel and hurried towards the door.

"Will you be back?" Katie asked.

Jill shook her head.

"I don't feel so well. I uh—I'll be back tomorrow."

Though Jill wished that her job did not affect her, it did. She worried about each and every teenager she worked with, especially ones as troubled as Brandon Schwartz. She desperately wanted to get through to him, and since his parents withdrew him from the school, she never would have the chance.

She wanted to spend the rest of her afternoon eating ice cream and watching chick flicks with Bo-Bo. She wanted to hide from the outside world, at least for the rest of the day. Failure was not an option when it came to her career. The kids needed her.

Her telephone began to ring again. It was most likely the school.

"What do you think, Bo-Bo?" she asked from her spot on the couch. "Think I should get it?"

He looked up at her with his big, brown eyes and let out a small whine.

"Yeah, I don't think so either, buddy."

She curled up, a pint of ice cream in her hands, and she let it ring. St. Margaret's had already ruined her day. She was not going to give the school the chance to ruin it any further.

It was not until several hours later that a knock on the door awoke her. Bewildered by her ability to sleep through the echo of the surround sound, her eyes flickered open.

Knock, knock, knock.

"Coming!" she yelled, scratching the back of her head. She swung her legs over the side of the couch and added, "One minute!"

Her eyes found the melted contents in the pint container and she made a face. She stood up, grabbed it, and dropped it in the trash on her way to the front door.

Knock, knock, knock.

"I said I'm coming!" Jill shouted, opening the door.

When she saw who was on the other side, her face fell.

"A-Adam!" she stammered. "What a—what a surprise! Um, what are you doing here? Door-to-door autographs?"

Adam chuckled and shook his head.

"No, nothing like that. I uh—I stopped at St. Margaret's to see if you were in but the girl in the office said you went home. Wanted to see how you were doing," he explained. "Well, it looks like you're kind of busy, so I suppose I ought to get going..."

Jill frowned and looked down at her feet.

"I'm not busy. Just a rough day at the office. Decided to take a sick day. You know how it is."

Adam smiled and nodded.

"Yeah. I do. So uh—you still live here, eh?"

Jill looked around the house and nodded.

"Yep. Grandpa gave it to me when he passed away. My mom moved into a place in town," she replied. "How'd you find me, anyway?"

Adam chuckled.

"Wasn't too hard to get the girl in the office to give me your address. If I knew you didn't move, I could've found it without the address," he explained. "I just figured after all these years..."

"You figured I would've moved on. Like you," Jill finished, awkwardly.

Adam looked down at the ground.

"Well, no, but—"

"Don't worry about it," Jill interjected. "So did you really just come here to see if I was okay? Or is there more to it?"

He laughed, nervously.

"Well actually, I wanted to talk. I mean...if that's okay."

Jill sucked on her teeth. Part of her did not want to give him the time of day.

"I guess. But make it quick."

She turned on her heel and started making her way towards the kitchen. When she noticed Adam was not behind her, she called him in.

"Are you coming or what?" she shouted. "I don't have all day!"

"O-oh! Yeah, I'm coming!"

His face flushed and he followed her inside. The screen door creaked closed behind him.

"Do you want an iced tea? Coffee? Anything?" Jill asked, shuffling through her refrigerator. "I have some orange juice if—"

"No, no. I'm fine," Adam interrupted, leaning against the counter. "Look, I don't want to impose or anything, so I'm going to make this quick."

Jill raised her eyebrows and tucked her long, blonde hair behind her ear.

"I'm listening."

Adam let out a deep sigh and scratched the back of his neck. Jill could sense his discomfort. Something was bothering him.

"Well, I just wanted to apologize—you know, for what happened between us."

"It was a long time ago, Adam," Jill murmured, her gaze averting towards the floor. "I've forgiven you."

"But I don't think you have," Adam said, darkly. "I think you're still mad at me, and honestly, who can blame you? I was a jerk. A huge jerk."

"Yeah. You were," Jill replied in a small voice.

"I know I can't take back everything I said, but I know now that I was wrong. For all of it. When I moved to the city, I thought

I knew what I wanted, but I didn't. I was naïve, Jill. Really naïve. The money, the women—it isn't worth it. None of it was worth it," Adam went on. "If cancer has taught me anything, it's to hold onto the things that matter. You mattered, Jill. We mattered. I know that I messed up any chance I had years ago, but I—I figured you at least deserved an apology."

While his words were beautiful, Jill was not sure whether he meant them or not.

"You knew exactly what to say when we were in high school, too," Jill noted. "Look how that turned out."

Adam nodded, holding his head lowly. He could not look her in the eye.

"I know. I'm a screw-up."

He ran his fingers through his hair and Jill noticed that his scalp appeared to be coming up. He pressed it back down with his fingertips. Jill's face flushed as she came to the realization that his perfect blond hair was not actually his at all. It was a wig.

"Well, you were a screw-up," she replied, reaching out to touch his arm. "It was really big of you to apologize to me. I appreciate it, Adam. I really do."

Adam smiled and nodded.

"Yeah. Yeah, it was no problem. Well uh, I suppose I should probably get out of here, huh?" he asked, nervously. He wandered back to the front door and pushed it open, only turning back to say, "It was nice talking, Jill."

Jill smiled.

"Yeah. It was."

Chapter Four – An Impromptu Brunch

Returning to St. Margaret's the next day was rather difficult for Jill. Not only had she left the previous day without much of an explanation, but she also had no idea how she was going to stay focused on work. Adam's visit had left her with more questions than answers and she was hardly prepared for a day full of meetings.

"Nice to see that you decided to show today," Katie murmured as Jill walked into the front office. "Feeling better?"

Jill nodded and replied, "Yes. Much."

"Good. Someone came in yesterday looking for you. An Adam—"

"He found me," Jill interjected. She pulled a quick smile and added, "Thanks."

She hurried towards her office and opened her daily planner. With back-to-back meetings all day long, she would have no time to think about Adam. Even though she wanted to push him to the back of her mind, she couldn't. She had waited for an apology for years. Finally, she had it, and she had no idea what to think.

There was a knock on the door.

"Ms. Goodman, I got an appointment with you," a voice grunted through the door. "Can I come in?"

Jill took a deep breath.

"Of course. Come in, Summer."

The door opened. The student frowned.

"It's Renée."

Jill peered into her planner and her face flushed.

"So it is!" she replied. "Please, sit down."

Renée snorted.

"Whatever."

By her third meeting, Jill was already starting to daydream.

"...and that's when Mr. Hofer told me that I had to take my nose ring out."

The student shifted in her seat, uncomfortably, staring at Jill for an answer.

"Ms. Goodman?" the student asked. "Ms. Goodman, are you okay?"

"O-oh, yes, Adrian. Sorry about that," she murmured, snapping back to reality. "So how did it make you feel when your parents found out that you failed that quiz?"

Adrian furrowed her brow.

"Angry, I guess? Didn't we already talk about that?"

"Oh yes, I'm sorry. What were you saying?"

"Ms. Goodman, we've been talking about my dress code violations for fifteen minutes now. Are you sure you're alright?" Adrian asked.

Jill looked up at her with watery eyes and smiled.

"I'm fine."

Suddenly, the PA buzzed. Jill listened closely.

"Ms. Goodman?" Katie asked, her voice drowned out by static.

Jill pressed the call button.

"Yes?"

"Ms. Goodman, you have a visitor. A Mr. Adam Panton. Should I send him down?"

Jill was surprised that Adam would show up at St. Margaret's again. Nevertheless, she pressed the call button and responded.

"Y-yeah. Send him down."

She let go of the button and turned to Adrian. Adrian seemed unimpressed.

"You can go back to class now, Adrian," she said. "We're done for the day."

Adrian rolled her eyes and slung her backpack over her shoulder. While Jill could have written her up for giving attitude, she decided not to. Her mind was on more important things.

Jill primped her hair in a tiny hand mirror as she waited for the knock.

A few moments later, it finally came. Her heart raced in her chest.

"Come in!" she sang.

Luckily, she sounded less nervous than she actually was.

"Hello, hello," Adam said, slowly opening the door. He flashed her a grin and added, "Am I interrupting?"

Jill raised her eyebrows and gestured one of the small plastic chairs.

"Not at all. Please, sit down."

"Don't mind if I do," he replied, lowering himself into the tiny chair. "Wow, these are smaller than I remember."

Jill giggled.

"Well, you are about forty more pounds than you were in high school."

"I am not," Adam joked, grabbing his gut. "Okay, maybe I am. Not for long, though!"

"You been working out?" Jill asked, leaning back in her desk chair.

Adam shook his head and whispered, "Not as much as I did in high school. Chemo tends to take the pounds off, though."

"Oh my—oh my goodness. I'm such an idiot. I'm sorry—"

"No, don't apologize," Adam interrupted, shaking his head. "I don't want pity. I just—I just wanted to see you."

Jill sat in silence for a minute. She was unsure what to say.

"I'm sorry, I didn't mean to—"

"Don't be," Jill interjected. She looked at the clock. "I have lunch in ten. If you could wait 'til then, we could go catch up."

Adam smiled.

"I'd like that."

Adam drove a modest SUV, which was far less than Jill expected. She found it cozy, though. She had never been impressed with money and materialism. When they were younger, that was all that Adam had to offer.

"So where's a good place for brunch in this town? Is Mack's still around?"

"That place will never shut down," Jill chuckled. "I can't believe you'd actually eat there. Remember when I suggested it for prom?"

Adam laughed as he stopped at one of the only three stoplights in town.

"Yeah, I'm pretty sure I told you I'd rather eat my own vomit. I was a real jerk when we were kids, huh?"

"Well, I wouldn't say that," Jill reassured him. "I think unappreciative would be a better word."

Adam frowned.

"That doesn't sound much better."

Jill didn't respond. They were pulling into the diner parking lot.

"Well, here we are," Adam said, coming to a stop in front of the building. "Ready for some steak and eggs?"

"I'm starving," Jill admitted. She laughed a little. "I don't think I could've eaten steak and eggs in front of you when we were teenagers."

Adam chuckled as he unfastened his seatbelt.

"You and your Caesar salad. No matter where we went."

"Well if you weren't always ogling at those girls in that catalog, I probably wouldn't have felt like I needed to lose weight," Jill pointed out. "But now, we aren't an item so I have no one to impress."

Adam smirked.

"You gonna stuff your face then?" he asked, opening his car door. "Am I gonna get to see Jill Goodman eat like a human for the first time in my life?"

Jill opened her door and stepped out.

"Maybe!" she yelled. "Only if you're paying!"

Adam laughed.

"Hey, just because I was cheap in high school doesn't mean I'm cheap now," he replied. "I've got you covered, okay?"

Jill blushed.

"Okay."

The grumpy-faced waitress came over to their table.

"How is your food?" she asked in a monotone grumble.

"Delicious," Adam said, his mouth full of eggs. "Way homier than anything I'd get in Salt Lake City."

"Good to hear," the waitress grumbled. "Refill on your coffee?"

Jill nodded and smiled.

"Please."

The waitress gave her a dirty look and seized her cup.

"I'll be back with that in a moment."

With the waitress out of her way, she could finally look into Adam's deep, green eyes. He grinned at her.

"I feel like I'm back in high school," he admitted. "Pretty girl that doesn't hate me. Middle-of-the-day breakfast."

"And is that a bad thing?" Jill asked, shoveling a forkful of steak and eggs into her mouth.

"I can't say it is," he replied with a smile. He looked around the diner and added, "I kind of missed this. Now that I'm back here, I really don't know what I was always running from."

Jill shrugged.

"You were young. A football star with the world ahead of you. What were you supposed to do?"

He looked her sharply in the eyes.

"A football star that was a massive idiot. College ball was fun, but if I knew it was going to cost me my relationship with you—"

"Save it, Adam," Jill intervened.

The waitress slipped her cup of coffee in front of her, along with the check. They had not even asked for it.

"Whenever you're ready," she whispered before slipping away.

"Jill, I'm trying to apologize for everything that I did. Can't you just get that?"

Jill sucked on her teeth and asked, "Are you apologizing for me or for your ego? Because I forgave you already. You don't need to keep talking about it. It was a long time ago."

"But I want to explain—"

"I don't need an explanation. You wanted the girls, the college life, the drinking. I stayed here and we grew apart. It's as simple as that," Jill interrupted. "If you really cared about me, you wouldn't have left. Now, I get that you're sick and you're trying to make amends before... Well, you know."

"No, I don't know," Adam replied, leaning back and crossing his arms. "Please, enlighten me. Tell me what you know about me that I don't know, because the Adam that I know—the new Adam—means what he says."

Jill looked down at her coffee as she stirred it. She could not look into those green eyes.

"It just seems kind of strange that you're all of a sudden back in town. Wanting brunch. The apology. It all seems really rushed," she murmured. "Considering your situation, it just seems like you're...I don't know. Forget it."

"What are you trying to say, Jill? That I'm just apologizing to you to get into God's good graces when I die? Is that what you're getting at?" he growled, seizing the check.

"No, that's not what I'm saying at all—"

"I think it is, actually," Adam cut her off. He opened his wallet and tucked some cash inside of it. "Look, I need to be getting home. Grab your things. I'll drop you off at St. Margaret's."

"But, Adam—"

"But what, Jill? You got anything else you'd like to say about how much of a jerk I am or can we ride back to the school in peace?" he asked, snidely.

She was speechless.

"You know, I've changed and maybe you have too. But maybe I changed for the better and you changed for the worst. The Jill I knew was forgiving, and kind. This Jill is cold and distant, sarcastic and dishonest. I'd take high school Jill any day," Adam said. He looked at the clock and lowered his voice. "Grab your purse. You're gonna be late."

Chapter Five – Regret

Jill was running out of sick days. According to her contract, she was only allowed to take five days off without a note from a doctor. After her altercation with Adam, she could hardly even finish her workday. The next morning, she decided to call in sick. She had no idea that a high school boyfriend could take such a toll on her.

She spent most of her days eating ice cream, curled up on the couch with Bo-Bo. Sometimes, she would pray for Adam's health. Part of her wanted to pray that he could forgive her, but she felt like that cheapened her relationship with God. Perhaps, there was a reason that she and Adam fought.

The phone had been ringing off the hook ever since Adam had been in town. Since she disconnected her answering machine, she just assumed it was her mother. She could have checked the caller ID, but something kept her from doing so. Instead, she moped on the sofa, watching TV and wishing that her career was not going down the drain. The world was collapsing in on her and there was nothing she could do about it.

Knock, knock, knock

Jill frowned. She had no idea who would be showing up at her house, but she certainly hoped that it was nobody from the school. Before getting up to answer it, she tousled her hair a little and practiced her fake sniffling.

She wrapped herself in her crocheted blanket and shuffled her feet towards the door, silently praying that it was not a coworker. When she opened the door, she saw that it was certainly not a coworker, but it still was not necessarily someone she wanted to see.

"O-oh. Adam. Hi. I uh—I wasn't expecting you."

"Well, you weren't answering your phone," he said, stepping inside. "You weren't at St. Margaret's. I figured you'd have to be here."

Jill closed the door behind him and nodded.

"Well, you caught me," she said, sitting down at the kitchen table. "So did you come to tell me how much of an idiot I am before you left for Salt Lake City?"

Adam laughed and shook his head, pulling out a chair to sit across from her. For a moment, Jill pictured him eating meals with her there—like a family. She shook off the notion as quickly as she could.

"Not quite," he said. "I actually came to tell you that uh—I'm going to be staying in town. For awhile. My doctors are here. My family is here. It just makes sense to stay right now. I know you probably don't care but I wanted to tell you."

Jill stared at the wood grain in the table. She was doing all she could to avoid his gaze.

"I see," she said. "So you're going to be getting treatment at Lenn Med?"

He nodded.

"Yeah. They have a pretty good oncologist there that really knows what she's doing. I'll just be staying with my parents for awhile 'til I find something, but maybe I'll move back for good. Salt Lake City was an adventure, but I'm not in my twenties anymore. I think it's time for me to settle down."

"Settle down," Jill repeated. "Well, that probably would be best. You need to relax right now. When the cancer got my dad, he needed rest. Lots of it."

Adam ran his fingers through his wig.

"Yeah, I've been feeling tired," he admitted. He leaned back and asked, "You know where I was when I first figured it out?"

Jill frowned.

"Where?"

"A nightclub," he replied, airily. "I went to the bathroom, started coughing and I couldn't stop. There was a whole handful of it—blood. I'd been drinking. I'd been partying. I had no idea what could've been causing it, but it was the last night I ever drank. If cancer has taught me one thing, it's that I'm not supposed to take life for granted. I uh—I was. I was taking it for granted. I wasn't going to church. There were a lot of women. I was a football star and I thought I was all that. Cancer taught me that I'm not."

His words were heavy. They sat there for a moment, in silence.

"I'm sorry," Jill finally said, looking up at him. "Nobody should have to find out that way."

"Yeah, maybe not. Maybe I get to take advantage of everything I've learned, though. The Lord works in mysterious ways. I mean, he brought us back together, didn't he?"

Jill's face flushed.

"Well, I don't mean together together," Adam corrected himself. "I just—I'm here and you're here and—"

Jill smiled and shook her head.

"Shush. You don't need to explain yourself. I'm glad you came. I really missed you, Adam. The good part of you. I know you seem to think that all I remember was the bad, but there were a lot of great things about our relationship too. I wouldn't mind a chance finding those things again. You know, now that we're more mature and all," she explained. She reached out and touched his hand. "I want to be here for you during all this."

Adam smiled at her.

"And if you had the chance to do that, what could happen?"

Jill laughed and leaned forward a little.

"I don't know. What would you want to happen?"

Staring into each other's eyes, they drew closer and closer. Adam never answered her with words, but as he pressed his lips against hers, the world finally felt like it made sense. She felt her face become hot as he caressed her cheek.

"Well, if that's what's going to be happening, I think I made the right decision letting you in."

Adam chuckled.

"You weren't gonna let me in?" he asked. "Were you really that mad at me?"

Jill shook her head.

"I thought you were someone from the school. Something told me to open the door, though."

Adam looked up.

"Divine intervention, maybe," he joked. "Now, how are you gonna balance a boyfriend in chemotherapy and taking care of all those kids at the school, huh?"

"Boyfriend?" Jill asked, raising an eyebrow. "Since when did I agree to that?"

"Oh, so you don't wanna be my girlfriend?" he asked, laughing a little. "Fine, then!"

"I'm just kidding!" Jill laughed. "Besides, you don't need any more pressure right now. And I don't either. Let's just be honest this time around. No games."

Adam nodded.

"We're not in high school anymore, Jill. Games are for boys. I'm a man."

"Well, you played a lot of them back then, so you're going to have to prove it to me."

Adam raised his brows.

"Oh? And how can I do that?"

Jill pecked his lips and smiled.

"With time, Adam. With time."

NOW I LAY ME DOWN TO WEEP

WENDY STEARNS

Now I Lay Me Down to Weep

The bell was chiming again, wearing on Carolyn's already frazzled nerves. Now what does he want? I was just there! Carolyn set down her book and hurried toward the back bedroom. Her father was laying in the bed as she had left him, his breaths short and raspy. She immediately checked the dialysis machine. Content it was functioning properly, she forced a smile upon her face and turned to face the gray faced man sunken into the pillows.

"Yes dad?"

"Carolyn, I need you to go into my desk in the study and get my will." She swallowed the lump in her throat.

"Dad, stop being so fatalistic," she pleaded. "You have beaten the odds before. You will do it again."

"Don't argue with me, girl. Just do what I say. It's in the top..." he trailed off and Carolyn's blue eyes widened. She rushed to his side. Exhaling slowly, she realized he was simply catching his breath.

"...top drawer," he continued as if he had not stopped. "It is the only document there. The key is in the safe. You know the combination. It's your mother's birthday." Why would you keep that as your password after all this time? Carolyn thought bitterly. You don't keep any other memory of her in this house.

She looked uncertainly at him and then toward the door as if deciding what to do.

"Go!" he urged. There was something in his tone which caused her to move. In moments, she was back, the papers in hand. Roger struggled to sit up and Carolyn rushed to assist him.

"Dad, you don't have to do this now," she implored. "Wait until you are feeling stronger."

"I won't be feeling stronger," he informed her with finality. "This is it."

Tears sprung into her eyes and Carolyn turned her head so he would not see her cry. He would be angered by her emotion. He had raised her to be strong, not show weakness.

"Carolyn! You better not be crying!" he growled. He began to cough at his strong words and she quickly shook her head.

"I'm not," she lied, willing away the water from her lids and smiling phonily. He reached out with a trembling hand and touched her arm, his weak fingers trying to squeeze her with affection but in his enfeebled condition, Carolyn could

only feel cold, lifeless fingers. He is already gone, she told herself. She could not stop the tears this time and she collapsed into a puddle of misery, burying her face in the crisp white sheets. The smell of death was in them. She knew it well.

"Stop!" Roger yelled, pounding his fists against the bed. "Stop! Look at me! Look at me! Look at me!"

"Look at me!"

Carolyn's head snapped up and she stared into the fierce brown eyes of Earl Sanders. His face was twisted into a look of disgust and he glared furiously at the nurse.

"What the hell are you doing in here? You can daydream on your own time! You've got no business doing it in here!" he barked at her. Carolyn shook off the memory and strolled further into the hospital room, a grim expression on her face.

"No need for such language, Mr. Sanders. I am here to check your vitals," she replied crisply, reaching out for his wrist. The emaciated man wrenched his arm back as if she was contagious.

"I'm not a guinea pig to be poked and prodded at!" he yelled. "You were just in here an hour ago!"

"And I will continue to come in every hour, sir." Earl spat and Carolyn narrowed her eyes, biting the insides of her cheeks to keep from losing her patience. *He knows he is dying. He is still in the anger stage. You must not allow your irritation to surface.*

"Nothing has changed," Earl snapped, settling back on the mound of pillows, eyeing Carolyn from his peripheral vision. "It doesn't matter how many times you run your useless tests. I'm still going be dead this time next week."

Carolyn cringed at his ruthless words, mostly because he was not entirely exaggerating.

"Now get out of here. You're not even a doctor!"

"I am a nurse practitioner, Mr. Sanders. I am the next best thing to a doctor that you're going to see today."

"I don't want the next best thing!" he snarled, picking up his water cup and hurling at Carolyn. "I want a real doctor. Get out!"

Sighing, Carolyn retreated from the room. There was no sense in arguing with the man. He was in his final stages of renal failure. He had been on a waiting list for five years for a new kidney, promised one twice and disappointed just as many times. Since he had joined the hospice two weeks earlier, not one person had come to visit him. His own wife, Sally Anne had passed only the previous year and Earl had no children. Carolyn was no stranger to death and the emotions which is stirred within its victims. Earl was fighting the good fight and nothing Carolyn or anyone else had to say would alleviate the hardship he was enduring. As she slowly descended the stairs to the main floor of the giant Victorian mansion, she nodded absently at a co-worker ascending the winding case.

"What's wrong, Carolyn?" Andy asked as he saw her face. She shook her dark hair, not wanting her voice to betray the sadness she was feeling. Since her own father had passed two months ago, the weight of work had seemed to suffocate her. Carolyn had been a hospice nurse for fifteen years and had always believed that the dying were the most in need of her services. Her reasoning had always been that when God decided it was time to accept them into his embrace, it was her calling to make the transition as painless as possible. She worked with her patients tirelessly to provide emotional as well as medical support. Yet since Roger had been taken from her, she had been considering another area of nursing. It all seemed for nothing. *Everyone dies. What's with all the preparation?* Her father's death had left an unfillable void in her heart, one that she felt would never stop aching. She found this puzzling since her relationship with Roger had always been strained.

"Carolyn?" She gulped back the misery in her throat and smiled weakly at Andy.

"No, nothing," she told the hospice director but the expression in his eyes told her that he wasn't buying into her claims.

"Who were you just visiting?" he pressed, turning to follow her back down the stairs.

"Earl Sanders." A look of understanding crossed over Andy's intelligent face and he gently steered Carolyn down the remaining steps and into the small area the staff used as their break room. He gestured for Carolyn to sit down and she grudgingly obliged. She was not in the mood to start a conversation with anyone at that moment but Andy was the house director and her boss essentially so Carolyn didn't see much of an opportunity for argument.

"Carolyn, may we have a discussion off the record?" he asked, closing the door to ensure for privacy. She nodded but she was battling myriad sarcastic thoughts running through her head. *Is this going to be a bonding boss moment where you tell me to 'hang in there?' and that 'things will get better if you give them time?' Because I really don't want to hear it, Andy.* Carolyn had been bombarded with platitudes since Roger had died and some days, other people's empty words were worse than the pain she was experiencing from her loss.

"Carolyn, you are hands down the best nurse we have here. I would say that you are the most qualified, compassionate medical staff I have ever encountered in my thirty years working in this field." Carolyn felt her eyebrow raise in surprise. *He doesn't look old enough to have been in any field for thirty years.* She did not speak and allowed him to finish his thought.

"Since you have joined us here at Hessler House, I can say that the palliative care the patients have received has been the best it has been in the ten years since it has been established."

Carolyn sighed. Under different circumstances, she likely would have appreciated the kind words but given her present situation, she wished Andy would get to the point so she could continue making her rounds.

"Thank you," she managed to utter but her voice lacked any sincerity. Andy leaned in toward her and Carolyn was surprised at the intimate motion.

"I have seen a change in your demeanor since your father has passed, Carolyn." Ice chips materialized in her veins and she whipped her head up to stare into his intense hazel eyes. *Oh Lord, is he firing me?* Her mind began to whirl, trying to recall what mistakes she had made over the past month since returning from her bereavement leave. *What have I done? Why can't I remember? Oh, please don't fire me! This job is all I have left. If I get fired, I won't get a job anywhere. I'll be a pariah in the field!* As if sensing her concern, Andy smiled and shook his head to ease her distressed look.

"Please don't look so stricken, Carolyn. I am simply stating an observation I have made since you have returned." Carolyn's concern abruptly turned to defensiveness.

"I have been under some stress," she replied tightly and Andy nodded.

"I understand that. And I want you to know that I am here if you need someone to talk to." Carolyn blinked, surprised by the sudden offer of friendship. She peered at him, lowering her guard slightly. In two years, she had developed a relationship of politeness with Andy, saying hello in passing, sharing the occasional cup of coffee but she would not have considered him more than an acquaintance. *He has very gentle eyes. I don't think I've ever sat this close to him before. I still wouldn't have guessed him to be in his fifties.*

"Thank you," she said again, unsure of how else to respond. She felt a slow flush building in her cheeks.

"I will try to be more focussed," she mumbled but as she said the words, she wasn't certain it was the truth.

"I didn't mean to imply that you weren't doing a wonderful job, Carolyn. On the contrary. Your work is beyond reproach. I just wanted to reach out to you. You are never alone." Carolyn shifted her eyes away, suddenly very conscious of his gaze upon her face.

"Also, I wanted to discuss Earl Sanders with you," Andy continued, settling back against the worn vinyl loveseat. Carolyn couldn't help but notice that the forest green in the sofa brought out khaki flecks in Andy's eyes. She cleared her throat, embarrassed by her thoughts and nodded. She hadn't realized she had been leaning in also and immediately righted her posture.

"There's nothing much to discuss," Carolyn said dryly. "He's dying and he's afraid. It isn't anything I haven't dealt with dozens of times in the past."

"Earl Sanders is a very difficult man," Andy said slowly. "He always has been. He and my father were in World War II together."

Carolyn was stunned by the information.

"He was a remarkable soldier, has enough accolades and medals to fill a museum. My father said that Earl once saved him from a certain prisoner of war situation by executing a daring rescue mission." Carolyn thought of the fragile old man laying in the bed upstairs and tried to envision him laying in a muddy, dangerous trench on Nazi territory. It hardly seemed fathomable but Carolyn did not doubt Andy's recount.

"He and my father remained friends throughout the war and when they got home, they both married and stayed in contact. Earl was a regular figure at our Sunday dinners and between him and my old man, they would regale us with wartime stories until our ears bled. But I think the war changed him. My father said that when they returned home, Earl was moody, sullen not at all like the jovial, happy-go-lucky man he had bonded with during the war."

Andy went silent for a moment and Carolyn cocked her head to the side.

"Why are you telling me this?" she asked finally. Andy chuckled softly.

"Maybe because I am a sentimental fool but the man upstairs is suffering inside and he needs to come to peace with whatever it is which is plaguing him before meeting our maker." The nurse began to nod slowly. *He is a man in pain, just as I am in pain.*

"I hope he will find the peace he is seeking," she told Andy earnestly.

"I think he will...provided you don't give up on him."

Carolyn rose to her feet, her mind processing what Andy had told her.

"Thank you, Andy," she told him, turning to leave.

"No, thank you, Carolyn. For everything you do."

As she left the break room, Carolyn realized she felt somewhat happy for the first time since her father had passed.

"Is he out there?"

Her dance instructor pulled the curtains aside and peered into the audience. Slowly, she withdrew her head and shook her blonde hair, a look of sympathy on her face.

"Not yet, Carolyn but I'm sure he'll be here soon," Miss Angie said with forced cheer. Disappointment flowed through her tiny frame with such force, Carolyn was afraid her knees would give way. Miss Angie was at her side, hugging her.

"He'll be here, Carolyn. Don't worry."

Sixteen-year-old Carolyn blinked quickly so her teacher would not see her expression. Her father had missed every recital that year. He would not be there. He never was. The music cued and Carolyn swallowed her bitter thoughts as she readied herself to enter the stage. Mom never missed any of my recitals. It's no wonder she left him. He was probably just as bad a husband as he is a father.

Earl Sanders was sound asleep in room 203 when Carolyn began her shift the following morning. It was barely the crack of dawn and she moved extra cautiously as to not disturb the man. Sleep was an elusive quality which had escaped Earl in the past months as he fought for his life. Despite his massive supply of pain medication, designed to lessen the symptoms of his debilitating illness, his insomnia would not ease. It was rare to see him in such as peaceful state and Carolyn had to watch him for a full minute to ensure that he was still breathing. Quietly, she paused by the wooden nightstand and lay several books at his side. She had wanted to be there to hand them to Earl personally but she dared not upset his slumber. *He will see these when he wakes. It will keep him entertained for a while.* On her tip toes, Carolyn turned to leave, smiling softly to herself. Suddenly Earl's voice rang out like a shot in a field.

"What did I tell you about coming in here, Nurse Wishes-She-Was-A-Doctor?"

Startled, Carolyn whipped around to face him.

"Oh, I'm sorry, Mr. Sanders, I didn't – "

"I didn't ask you for an apology! I asked you what you're doing in here!" Without speaking, Carolyn pointed at the bedside table, her eyes beseeching him to look. His inky eyes took on a look of stone and he peered at where her hand was pointed. If possible, his already wan face went more ashen.

"Where did you get those?" he demanded, fighting to sit up. Carolyn hurried over to assist him, concerned about his strength.

"I went online and did some research. It turns out you're a hero, Mr. Sanders," she fibbed as she adjusted his mound of pillows. He swatted her away as if she was a pesky gnat and reached for the books she had placed upon the platform.

"Have you got a hearing problem or something? I didn't ask you about me. I asked you where you got those books!"

"I bought them last night after I left here. I looked you up online and then there was a link to a Barnes and Noble directory where I could find you in print. It shows all of the battles you were in and – "

"I know what it shows!" To Carolyn's shock, Earl drew up one weak arm and feebly swiped at the pile of books, sending them flying to the floor. Carolyn reeled back, her hand flying to her mouth to hide a gasp.

"If I see you in here again, next time I won't be so nice!" Earl screamed, his face a mask of rage. Carolyn fled the room, sobs shaking her body as she flew down the winding staircase and out the door. In the sanctuary of her car she began to bawl, full body heaves of woe. *He's a monster. I don't care if he's dying. Who can treat other people like this?* She willed herself to take deep breaths and steady her shuddering body. *Dad. Dad treated people like this.*

"Carolyn, sit down." She walked into the living room, her knapsack still perched upon her slim shoulders. She adjusted her owl-like glasses and stared at her father. He was staring out the bay window in the living room.

"Can I just put my book bag upstairs?" she asked, worried that she was facing a punishment.

"No. Leave you bookbag. Sit down. I need to talk to you about something."

Very slowly, the seven-year-old ventured toward her intimidating father, lowering her pack to the floor.

"Don't leave it on the floor!" he snapped, turning away from his reverie. "Put it by the stairs."

Obediently, young Carolyn rushed to drop the bag on the steps to the backsplit and returned to where her father was pacing the floor.

"Your mother is gone," he said without preamble. Carolyn blinked uncomprehendingly at the stranger she called "dad."

"Gone where?" she questioned innocently. "To the store?"

"Don't ask stupid questions, Carolyn. I wouldn't be having a serious discussion with you if your mother had simply gone to the store, now would I?"

The child did not reply, her mind racing.

"Where did she go?" Carolyn asked meekly but she was terrified of the answer to come.

"I don't know. She left a note saying she wasn't coming back."

Tears slipped down the young girl's face and she stared up at her father.

"But why, dad? Why would she leave me?"

Roger shrugged and stopped pacing to regard his only daughter.

"Your mother has a lot of problems," he told her. "Stop crying. It won't bring her back."

Carolyn tried to wipe the streaks from her face but the tears continued to flow. Her father was growing angry.

"Stop it right now, Carolyn! You must not cry. You must be strong and always put on a brave face no matter how badly you feel inside. Do you understand?"

"Yes dad," she whispered but she didn't understand. She couldn't comprehend how her free-spirited, loving, fun mother would leave her alone with her rigid, overbearing father. She will be back for me, Carolyn told herself. She loves me. She would never leave me here with him forever.

But the days turned to weeks and the weeks, years. Madeline never returned nor did she ever contact her daughter. Carolyn was finally forced to accept that Madeline had left, tired of being suffocated by her husband and Carolyn could not blame her mother. She was tired of him too.

He is just like dad, Carolyn thought. She had finally collected herself and returned to the Hessler House. Inside one of the many bathrooms, she splashed cold water on her face and studied her reflection in the mirror. She saw so much of her father in her face and so little of Madeline. She no longer wore the huge eyeglasses, swapping them in for contact lenses as to not detract from her long lashed blue eyes. She had a mop of Roger's unruly chestnut hair and his skinny build. *I wish I had something of mom's,* Carolyn thought wistfully but was immediately ashamed by the thought. It was a rote idea, missing her mother. As the years passed, it had become harder and harder to remember what her mother looked like. Roger had either thrown out all her pictures or stored them somewhere that Carolyn would never locate them. Some nights, when Carolyn could not sleep, she would lay in bed trying desperately to hear her mother's voice saying something, anything to her but as time elapsed, Madeline's voice was as much a memory as her mother. Sighing, Carolyn redid the messy ponytail in her hair and exited the bathroom before she could acknowledge it looked worse than before. She decided to stay on the main floor for the remainder of her shift. She would have someone else tend to Earl Sanders. She was much too fragile to endure any more abuse from the man and she was just as concerned about his safety as she was about hers. With an hour left in her shift, a code blue came in on the second floor. Ginger Bellamy had passed away in room 201 and Carolyn was required to attend as the other hospice nurse was otherwise indisposed. The doctor quietly declared the death and Carolyn prepared Mrs. Bellamy for the arrival of the medical examiner. As Carolyn walked down the hall, she was intuitively aware she was about to pass Earl's room. She stepped up her gait when he called out to her.

"Hey! Nurse Next-Best-Thing-To-A-Doctor!" Carolyn was tempted to continue walking but there was something in his tone which suggested he was not on a tirade so she reluctantly stopped in the doorway. To her surprise, Earl was sitting up in bed, pouring through the books she had purchased on World War II. He waved a bony hand for her to enter but Carolyn remained in the doorway.

"Yes, Mr. Sanders?" she asked.

"Come in here a second. I want show you something in these books you bought for me," he replied, barely glancing up from his reading. Warily, Carolyn crossed the threshold toward him, prepared to run at the first hint of trouble.

"Have you got superhuman vision or something?" Earl barked. "You can't see anything from over there. Come closer."

Uncertainly, Carolyn glanced at the empty hall and then back at her patient. He did not seem threatening at that moment and it was her job to attend to him. On the contrary, in fact. He seemed to have lost twenty years off his appearance and he was smiling wistfully as if the books had put him into some sort of nostalgic time warp. Carolyn approached cautiously and glanced down where he was pointing. A glossy black and white picture of an army brigade smiled at her.

"That's me and my squad," he told her. "May of '42."

Carolyn drew in closer and peered at the photo more intently. Squinting, she could make out a very handsome Earl Sanders in a pair of army fatigues and white undershirt, a cigarette hanging out of his mouth. He looked carefree despite of his dire circumstances, grinning a charming, boyish smile. His arm was around another man who looked remarkably like Andy, the house director. As if reading her thoughts, Earl piped up.

"That snot nose brat who runs this joint? What's his name? Alfie? That's his papa, JonJon. Well, we used ta call him JonJon. His name is Jon." Carolyn found herself laughing, her initial nervousness slipping away.

"His name is Andy," Carolyn giggled but she seized the opportunity to keep him talking. "You still keep in touch with your army friends, Mr. Sanders?"

His head whipped up at her and he scowled.

"If you're going to poke and prod at me all day like some hamster in a cage, you can probably call me Earl," he snapped. "And aside from Jonny, no, they're all dead now. Or have dementia so no point in bugging them to discuss old times."

Carolyn thought she felt her heart break slightly. *No wonder he's so miserable. He has no one. He's going to die alone. Just like dad did.*

"Don't look at me with pity eyes, nursey. I had a good life," Earl told her, noticing the shadow which crossed over her blue irises.

"I'm sure you did, Earl. From what I can see, you've lived five lives. But surely there must be someone you want here with you, you know, someone to hold your hand..." Carolyn trailed off, suddenly embarrassed under his scrutinizing stare.

"For when I kick the bucket?" Carolyn grimaced at the word choice and glanced down at her white shoes.

To her surprise, he began to laugh.

"The only person I want with me has been gone for a long while," he told her, closing the book and sitting back. Carolyn wanted to kick herself for her insensitive comment. *The man just lost his wife. Good work reminding him of that in his darkest hour.*

"I'm sorry about your wife," she whispered, hanging her head. Again, Earl chortled and Carolyn stared at him, appalled by his reaction.

"Nah, I didn't mean Sally Anne, God rest her beautiful soul. But Sally Anne wasn't the love of my life." Carolyn found herself sitting, enthralled by Earl's brutally honest words. It was not surprising that he was pouring his heart out to her as near the end, patients often felt the need to unleash the burdens they kept deep in their soul but Carolyn was startled all the same.

"Who was the love of your life?" she pressed.

"Her name was Glenda Thompson and she was my entire world." Earl's face softened as he tried to recall the delicate features of the woman once he had obviously cared for very deeply. "She and I were joined at the hip from dawn until dusk every day since we were knee high to grasshoppers. We sat together in class, walked home from school together. She loved me more than anyone ever had before or did again."

"What happened to her, Earl?"

"I happened to her. While I wasn't old enough to be drafted, I wanted to serve my country but most of all, I was eighteen and scared. Maybe I thought I was too young to be tied down to one woman. Hindsight is always twenty-twenty, isn't it? I ran off to join the army and slunk off like a thief in the night without saying good-bye."

"Why?" Carolyn was aghast. "I thought she was the love of your life!"

Earl shrugged.

"Weren't you ever eighteen and scared? I was stupid. I spent my entire tour pining for her but I didn't write her once. I was a kid with stupid kid emotions and stupid kid thoughts. I thought when I get home, she'll still be there, waiting for me."

"She wasn't, was she?"

Earl shook his head and for a moment, Carolyn thought she saw tears mist his eyes.

"Nope. Married Jerry Malcom. That blockhead was the dumbest kid in our class. I swear she did it out of spite. We never spoke again but I'll tell you, Nurse,

I have never stopped thinking about the way that woman made me feel. I loved Sally Anne, truly I do but she never made my heart race like Glenda did. I was happy with my wife but I always wondered what became of Glenda Thompson." Earl's eyelids were getting heavy and Carolyn rose to her feet slowly.

"Get some rest, Earl. I'll be back tomorrow and you can tell me some more war stories, okay?"

"Hey, nursey," he called sluggishly. Carolyn turned to regard him.

"Yes Earl?"

"I'm sorry I was being such a jerk to you. It's just..."

"I know, Earl. No need to apologize. See you tomorrow, okay?" He was already falling asleep and Carolyn backed out of the room as he nodded slightly, acknowledging her words. Carolyn hurried toward Andy's office. *I must find Glenda Thompson before it's too late.*

She glanced up at the address again to confirm and then put the car in park. *This is a really bad idea,* she repeated to herself as she made her way up to the apartment building. *But Earl deserves some peace on his deathbed. You have to at least try to do this for Earl.* Inside, she stared at the names on the intercom. She jabbed at a button and waited, resisting the urge to run away and abort the mission altogether. Before she could do the sensible thing and leave, a woman's voice piped through the voice box.

"Yes?"

"Mrs. Malcom?"

A slight pause followed the question.

"Yes. Who is this?"

"My name is Carolyn Ward. I am a hospice nurse at Hessler House in Lafayette. Do you think we could speak for a moment?"

Instantly, the door buzzed to allow for Carolyn to enter and she ran up the third-floor walk-up to Glenda Malcom's apartment. Glenda was already standing in the hall in wait, a handsome older woman in her late eighties. As Carolyn searched her face, she could see how Earl would have been so smitten with her in his youth. She was a stunning combination of elegance and fire. She peered at Carolyn curiously before ushering her into her tiny dwelling.

"Welcome to my humble abode," Glenda said wryly, gesturing about the bachelor apartment.

"Do you live here alone?" Carolyn asked once they had been seated at the small kitchen table which doubled as a coffee and sofa table.

"Since my divorce twenty years ago, yes," Glenda conceded. "Don't need much more than this at my age."

"You're divorced from Jerry Malcom?" Carolyn could hardly believe what she was hearing. Glenda's eyes narrowed at the sound of her ex-husband's name.

"Yes. I'm sorry, what are you doing here?" she demanded, her tone slightly frosty.

"I am a nurse at Hessler House. It is a hospice in Lafayette. One of my patients used to be...acquainted with you," Carolyn faltered. Glenda Malcom sat back, a suspicious expression in her face.

"If this is some kind of catfish scam, lady, you can't take me for anything," she snapped and Carolyn almost laughed. "My grandkids have me wired on the interweb and I haven't got a nickel to part with."

"No, ma'am. My patient's name is Earl Sanders. Do you remember him?"

As if a light had been switched on in her face, Glenda's expression exploded into excitement.

"Early? You know Early?" she cried, leaning forward to grasp Carolyn's hands. The nurse nodded and then watched as the happiness drained from her face.

"Wait, didn't you say you're from a hospice? He's dying?" she whispered and Carolyn bobbed her head again, hanging her head.

"I was hoping you would come with me back to the house so he can see you one last time. I fear you are his one who got away," Carolyn told her gently and Glenda nodded immediately rising to her feet.

"Although God knows he doesn't deserve it, leaving me all those millions of years ago!"

"He has regretted it every day for seventy years, Glenda."

"He better have!" she shouted, locking the door and hurrying after Carolyn.

Earl was asleep when Carolyn brought Glenda to the hospice. It was early evening and as they approached his bed, there was something about his expression which instantly alarmed Carolyn. She pressed the call button by his bed.

"What's wrong?" Glenda screeched. "Is he dead?"

"No, no, Mrs. Malcom. He's alive," Carolyn assured her but her heart was racing as she recognized something in Earl's serene face. The night nurse arrived.

"Has he passed, Carolyn?" Sandra asked, rushing toward Earl but Carolyn shook her head.

"No, Sandy. Why is he still sleeping?" she asked but in her heart, she already knew the answer. Sandra blinked and stared at Carolyn.

"He has been sedated because of his agitation. The delirium hasn't set in from pain so we had to put him under."

"Under?" Glenda yelled. "What do you mean? Wake him up! I want to talk to him and tell him how much I have missed him all of these years! I want him to know that I married the wrong man and I should have waited for him! I want him to know I've always loved him!"

Carolyn swallowed the lump in her throat and shook her head miserably. She had been too late.

"It's too late," she whispered. "He is in a coma and will remain in one until he passes. It is the most painless way for him to go."

Glenda let out an anguished cry, a feral, penetrating sound which pierced the hearts of everyone in earshot.

"No! Earl, I'm sorry! I've always loved you! Early, wake up, please!"

Carolyn put her hand gently on Glenda's shoulder as her face fell into the sheets. The old woman grasped his hand tightly.

"He knows," Carolyn whispered. "He has always known."

"Stop your crying, Carolyn, stop it!"

"Dad, I can't! You're dying and I can't watch this!"

She turned and ran from the house, leaving the door wide open in her wake. She could not watch him suffering, could not handle the thought of tending to his corpse. She collapsed on the front lawn and curled into a ball. Mom, why did you leave us? I need you to help me through this? How could you leave me alone with him for all of this time? I can't do this! Carolyn sat up suddenly, realizing what she had done and scrambled back into the house. Roger lay in his bed, his eyes open in a perpetual stare of eternal sleep, clutching a letter in his hand. Choking on her sobs, Carolyn retrieved the note and read it.

Dear Carolyn,

I know you have always thought me to be a harsh and demanding man, especially in the absence of your mother. I always tried my best to shield you from the realities of who your mother was while providing for you. I missed your childhood because I was working, endlessly working. You may not recall but I often did sixty or seventy hour weeks. Your mother accumulated a mountain of debt in our names before she disappeared with the neighbor's son. I quietly paid for the neighbor to move so that the scandal would not ever reach your ears. I lived in constant fear that you would hear about Madeline's drunken escapades with other men, some of them young enough to be her own child. I lived in constant fear that you would turn to the bottle yourself one day as you always wore the same expression of melancholy which she did. I lived in constant fear that you would abandon me, just as she did and God knows, I tried every way I knew how to ensure none of these things occurred. Yes, I was tough on you but I was tougher on myself. I have always loved you very much and perhaps I did not show it when I was alive but I hope that in my death you can understand why I did what I did.

Until the pearly gates reunite us once more,

Daddy

The sun was shining and the birds singing a squabbling song above the cemetery when Carolyn approached with the roses. Leaning over, she wiped dirt off the epitaph and lay the flowers on the grave. It was the first time she had come since his death and she didn't know what to say. Pausing, she looked to the heavens as if expecting the word of God to guide her. Suddenly a smile, a true, genuine beam lit her face as if she had an epiphany and she looked down at where her father was laying to rest.

"I forgive you, dad," she whispered, turning away. Fifty yards away, under a weeping willow tree, Andy held out his hand.

"Are you ready?" he asked. *Yes. Yes, I am ready to move on now,* she told herself. Nodding, she accepted his outstretched palm and the two headed off into the sunlight.